JAYME'S JOURNEY

A CHRISTIAN ROMANTIC SUSPENSE

LAURA SCOTT

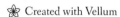

CHAPTER ONE

The pungent scent of smoke pulled Jayme Weston from sleep.

Fire!

She bolted upright in bed, her heart pounding, fear clawing up her back. She swept her gaze frantically over the room, searching for the yellow and orange flames. It took a moment for her to register that the fire was from her dreams.

Her nightmares.

Swallowing hard, she pressed a hand to her chest and willed her pulse to slow down. She instinctively massaged her scarred hand, bending her fingers back and forth. But then she wrinkled her nose again.

The smoke scent lingered. Maybe even getting stronger.

It wasn't her imagination!

Jayme scrambled out of bed, jammed her feet into running shoes, and pulled a sweatshirt on over her sleepshirt and shorts. She grabbed her phone and a large baseball bat. She was grateful Caitlyn had moved out with her college friend at the start of the semester. Yet being alone in the small house only emphasized her vulnerability.

Never again, she thought grimly as she gripped the bat and tiptoed down the short hallway to the living space. She wasn't a victim, she was a strong and capable woman. The smoke scent was stronger now, a haze hanging in the room. But she still couldn't see any sign of an actual fire. And the smoke wasn't enough to trigger the alarm.

Yet she wasn't going to take any chances either. She swept her thumb across the phone screen and quickly dialed 911. When the operator answered, Jayme did her best to remain calm.

"My name is Jayme Weston. I live on Oakdale Road in Sevierville, and I smell smoke inside my house. I don't see a fire, but I would like you to send the fire department out to investigate."

"What's the house number?"

Jayme relayed the information, still searching for the source of the smoke. Was she making a big deal out of nothing? Maybe the fire was somewhere nearby and not actually in her home. They hadn't had a lot of rain recently, so it could be that a portion of the woods was burning. And it would explain why her smoke detectors weren't going off.

"Ma'am, are you able to get out of the house?" the dispatcher asked.

On cue, the smoke detector in her living room began to blare loudly. She winced and shouted into the phone. "Yes!" Tucking the bat beneath her arm, she grabbed her purse off the counter and ran to the front door. Outside, it was easier to hear the dispatcher. "I didn't see any flames."

"The fire could be in the attic or basement. Please stay outside, far enough back to remain safe. I've sent the fire department to your location."

The fire might be in the attic or basement? The basement was empty except for the washer and dryer. Jayme glanced up at the roof of her house. There was no indication the fire was in the attic, yet she wasn't an expert on house fires.

Although she had started one. A long, long time ago.

Taking a deep breath of fresh air, she shoved the old memories away. She stumbled across the lawn, glancing back over her shoulder at the house.

She hadn't turned on any lights, so it was completely dark, with no sign of anything amiss.

But the smoke had to have come from somewhere. She was tempted to run around to the backyard to see if she could figure out where the smoke was coming from, but the wail of sirens convinced her help was on the way.

The early October air was relatively cool, especially at night. Maybe she should have changed into jeans; her legs were chilled. She dropped the baseball bat, convinced she didn't need it, and wrapped her arms around herself, trying to stop from shaking. A reaction to the smoke and her dream of the fire rather than to the cool temperatures. The scent of smoke clung to her clothing, reassuring her that it was real. Not some figment of her overactive imagination. And the smoke detectors were still screeching.

The sirens grew louder, overwhelming the annoying chirp of the smoke detector. Soon she could see the swirling red lights cutting through the darkness. The fire department had made good time. Granted, Sevierville wasn't that large, and it wasn't that late, just past midnight.

She felt silly standing out on the sidewalk next to her baseball bat. But the team of firefighters pretty much ignored her as the fire engine pulled up in front of her house. They jumped down and spread out around her property. They were all dressed from head to toe in heavy coats, hats, and carrying a lot of gear. One of them crossed directly to her. "Are you Jayme Weston, the homeowner? You called about smelling smoke?"

"Yes, the smoke woke me from a sound sleep, and you can hear the detector going off. I looked around and could see a haze in the house, but no source of the fire." She rubbed her hands over her arms. "Is there a forest fire nearby that may have caused this? It doesn't look to me like my house is on fire."

"No other fires have been reported nearby. Please stay back, we'll take a look." The firefighter lifted a hand and gestured toward the door. Two firefighters went inside while he and another firefighter walked around the outside of her property.

A few of her neighbors' lights flipped on, no doubt woken by the sound of the fire truck. She glanced around, noticing faces pressed against the windows. Her cheeks flushed, and she ran her fingers through her red hair. This was going to be mighty embarrassing if it turned out to be a false alarm.

Her closest neighbor, Mrs. Katz, hurried outside. "Jayme dear, are you okay?"

"I'm fine." Mrs. Katz had a kind heart and certainly meant well, but she was also extremely nosy. Jayme forced a smile. "No need to be concerned. I'm sure it's nothing."

"Well, the fire department must be here for *something*," the woman insisted. "I'm glad you're okay, though." Despite her nosiness, Jayme did her best to stay on good terms with the woman. Mrs. Katz had often treated Caitlyn like a granddaughter.

Her experience of living with family was limited to the foster homes she'd been in. The last one in particular she'd suffered physical and emotional abuse. And more. There was no point in dredging up the past now, but she edged closer to Mrs. Katz, once again grateful not to be alone. "Did you happen to smell smoke?"

"No, dear. Is that what this is about?" Mrs. Katz's eyes widened with interest as she scanned the area. "I don't see any sign of fire."

"I didn't either." She lifted her arm to Mrs. Katz's face. "But you can smell the smoke clinging to my clothes, right?"

Mrs. Katz sniffed. "Yes. That's so strange. Maybe a part of the woods is on fire?"

"But we'd see the flames, wouldn't we? And the firefighters would have known about that."

"Over here," a voice shouted.

Her heart leapt into her throat, and she found herself gripping Mrs. Katz's arm. Had they found something?

Jayme watched as a fireman pulled the long hose toward the right side of her house. It didn't take long for the crew to douse whatever they'd found, and within minutes, the crew had brought the hose back and returned to the fire truck.

Maybe she'd woken up just in time. Calling for the firefighters, who'd found the source before it had time to spin out of control. Thank goodness for smoke detectors.

The same firefighter who'd spoken to her on arrival came over to join her. For once, she didn't mind Mrs. Katz hanging around. "Ms. Weston? We found the source of the fire."

"Where? Is my house damaged?"

"Not from what we can tell. The fire was found outside the east part of your home near the heating vent. That's how the smoke was sucked into your house."

Jayme frowned. "But I don't understand. What was burning? Did my furnace malfunction?"

"No." The firefighter took her arm and drew her away from Mrs. Katz. He lowered his voice and said, "Ms.

Weston, you need to know I've called in the arson investigator. The fire was small, but it was also deliberately set."

She blinked, wondering if she'd misheard him. "Deliberately set? Are you sure?"

"Positive." There was no room for debate in his tone.

"But—who would do such a thing? Kids?"

The firefighter shrugged, eyeing her steadily. "I don't think it was kids. The fire was set in a way that it wouldn't spread but would cause enough smoke to be sucked into your home to be noticeable."

A shiver snaked down her spine. That certainly didn't sound like something kids would do. She cleared her throat, striving to remain calm. "I'm glad it wasn't more serious, but please tell me, have you seen this happen anywhere else?"

"No. And I haven't heard about it either. That's the reason I called the arson investigator. Lincoln Quade covers the entire city, among others, and would know if this particular type of signature had been used anywhere else recently."

Signature? It sounded like something out of a movie. She nodded dumbly, grappling with what he was telling her. The fire had been set on purpose, but only enough to cause smoke to fill her home, to set off the smoke detectors, but not enough to engulf the house in a huge blaze.

It didn't make any sense. The firefighter must be wrong; this particular incident had to be something a bored teenager had come up with.

"Oh, there's Linc now," the firefighter said.

Jayme saw the twin headlights grow bright as a large SUV pulled over to park near the large fire truck. When the firefighter she'd been talking with crossed the yard to meet up with the driver, she followed more slowly, in no hurry to join them. She veered back toward the sidewalk where Mrs. Katz was standing.

Watching the two men speak in low tones was easier than trying to understand what had happened here. They walked over to the side of the house where her air-conditioning unit was located.

"Is everything all right, dear?" Mrs. Katz asked.

"Yes, everything is fine." She forced a smile. "Apparently, it was a small fire set by kids. It made a lot of smoke but didn't cause any real damage." She patted the woman on the shoulder. "Nothing for you to worry about, Mrs. Katz."

"Kids?" Mrs. Katz tsked. "I just don't understand this new generation."

Jayme smiled. "Me either." She was twenty-nine years old but felt decades older. Living in the woods, then on the streets while caring for Caitlyn had forced her to grow up real fast.

Too fast.

But Mrs. Katz didn't need to know that. "Get some sleep, Mrs. Katz. The fire is out, and we're all safe. That's what matters."

"Of course, dear." The woman's curious gaze darted back to where the men were still talking. "Jayme, if you need a place to stay, you're welcome at my house."

"Thank you, that's very sweet." Jayme was truly touched by her hospitality. She knew from personal experience that not everyone would have made the offer. "But since the fire was outside and didn't cause any damage, I'll be fine."

"If you're sure." Mrs. Katz gazed around with frank curiosity, clearly not satisfied there'd been enough drama.

"I'm sure. Get some rest." Jayme moved away, walking

over to where the arson investigator and the firefighter were talking. The two men had large flashlights they used to illuminate the area. Even as she approached, she could see the black soot, which had been caused by the fire, staining the white siding of her house.

Thankfully, it wasn't anything worse than a black sooty stain. Nothing like the cabin she and the other foster kids had watched go up in flames thirteen years ago.

"Clever setup," a deep male voice said. "Thanks for calling me in."

"Figured you'd want to know." The firefighter caught sight of her. "Linc, this is Ms. Jayme Weston, she's the homeowner."

"Linc Quade, arson investigator." The tall man shifted his flashlight and offered his hand. She forced herself to take it, ignoring the way his fingers wrapped around her scarred hand. She didn't doubt he could feel the raised burn scars. "Ms. Weston, can we go inside to talk?"

"I—uh, sure." She hadn't expected that. "I assume the house is safe for me to go inside?"

"Yes, it's safe. The remaining smoke should dissipate soon. There wasn't enough to cause any real damage."

She let out a tiny breath. "Good to know."

"Shall we?" Linc Quade seemed anxious to get her away from the scene of the fire. Maybe he was worried she'd mess up any remaining evidence.

She walked across her dew-damp lawn, took a moment to scoop up her baseball bat, and led the way inside, flipping on the lights, which were bright enough to hurt her eyes. The smoke detectors were still blaring, but the fire investigator quickly reset them. She crossed over to the small kitchen table. Up close, she could see Linc Quade's handsome features more clearly. His blond hair was cut military short, a shadow of scruff covered his cheeks as if he hadn't shaved in a day or so, and his piercing dark eyes were intense enough to knock her off-kilter. She set the bat down, turned away, and tried to focus. "Ah, do you want some coffee?"

"No thanks." He was polite as he gestured for her to sit before dropping into the chair across from her. For a long moment, he simply looked at her. "As you've already been told, we know the fire was set on purpose."

"So I hear. Kids, right?"

"Not likely." Linc Quade stared at her for another long moment, then his gaze dropped to her scarred hand and wrist. "Looks like this isn't your first close encounter with a fire."

She instinctively covered the scars with her uninjured hand as if that alone would make them disappear. "That was from an accident thirteen years ago."

"What happened?"

Jayme shifted in her seat, unsure why he was asking about the past. "Does it matter? Thirteen years is a long time, and that event doesn't have anything to do with today."

He leaned forward, propping his elbows on the table. "Ms. Weston, I've been investigating fires for over three years now. I'm the best judge of what matters and what doesn't."

She wanted to snap but managed to control her redheaded temper. Since he didn't seem willing to let it go, she decided to give him the bare minimum information. Even telling him that much wouldn't be easy. Caitlyn was the only person who knew the varnished truth about what happened that night in the Preacher's cabin, and as far as she was concerned, that was one person too many. No one else needed to hear the gory details. She held Linc's dark brown gaze. "I accidentally broke an oil lantern, and some of the hot oil spilled on my hand and wrist."

He surprised her by reaching across the table to lightly grasp her injured hand. He examined it closely. Why on earth she noticed the gentle strength in his fingers was beyond her. "Thirteen years ago? These scars are pretty bad. Why didn't you get appropriate care?"

Linc Quade knew far too much about fires and burns for her peace of mind. "I was too far away from civilization when this happened. By the time I was able to get anywhere close to a place offering medical care, it was too late." She tugged her hand from his, gripping her hands tightly in her lap. "Why don't you explain to me why my injury from thirteen years ago matters?"

His dark gaze bored into hers. "Sometimes victims of fire become obsessed with fire, sometimes referred to as the dancing dragon. It wouldn't be the first time a fire victim became an arsonist."

Never in her life had she heard of fire called the dancing dragon. Then the rest of his words registered, and her jaw dropped in shock. "Me? You think I started the fire outside my own house? That's ridiculous. Why would I do that, then call you? Especially when I'm terrified of fire."

He shrugged. "Why are you terrified of fire? I thought the burn on your hand was from hot oil?"

She felt like he'd punched her in the gut. He was smart, she'd give him that.

Or maybe she was an idiot to think she could fool him. The spilled oil had in fact started a fire. That night thirteen years ago was seared painfully in her mind. The Preacher, as he called himself, had ranted and raved at the foster kids in his care, screaming about how they were all going to hell for being terrible sinners. He'd hit them with switches to hammer the point home.

If that wasn't bad enough, he'd set his sights on her. The evil leer in his gaze when he looked at her chest, her thighs made her want to throw up. She had no idea what to do, how to keep him from acting on his sick attraction, but escape was impossible.

When he made his move, she'd been grossly unprepared. He grabbed her, dragged her down, and began unfastening his pants. Horrified by what he was trying to do, she tried to call out to wake Ruth, but the woman was sleeping as if she'd been drugged.

And maybe she had been.

Panicked, she'd grabbed the oil lantern and swung it at the Preacher in an effort to get away. The oil had burned her hand, but she hadn't noticed because the Preacher screamed in agony as the hot oil burned the side of his face and his chest. Seconds later, the sofa erupted into flames as the Preacher stumbled toward the bedroom in an effort to save himself.

That moment she knew she needed to get away, no matter what. Ignoring her burns, she'd rushed over to yank up the cellar door, which was where they were forced to sleep. She'd been surprised to see Sawyer and Hailey already at the top of the stairs. Jayme had helped them up and out of the cellar. By the time they'd stumbled outside, the cabin was engulfed in thick smoke and flames. Coughing, nearly gagging, they managed to survive the fire by running and hiding in the woods.

The Preacher and Ruth, however, hadn't made it out of the fire.

"Ms. Weston?" His deep voice drew her from her troubled thoughts. "Are you okay? You look upset."

Upset was putting it mildly. Jayme squared her shoulders and met his gaze head-on. "I'm not upset," she lied. "And yes, if you must know, the hot oil did cause a small fire. Thankfully, I managed to escape without a problem. Only my right hand and wrist were burned." She tried to smile, but it felt like her face was frozen. "Please be assured that I am not obsessed with fire. And I did not set the fire outside my own house. I would never do something like that. In fact, I took the baseball bat with me in case the person who did this was hanging around nearby." She rose to her feet. "If that's all, I think it's best if you leave."

Linc slid his business card across the table and rose, forcing her to tip her head back to look up at him. The man was tall, well over six feet, and came across as rather intimidating. Still, she hadn't survived in the wilderness without being strong, so she simply tilted her chin and stayed right where she was. His dark eyes seemed to look right through her to the hidden secrets she'd buried deep within.

"Ms. Weston, my only goal is to uncover the truth about what happened here."

"I'm happy to hear that because it's a goal we share. I sincerely hope you can find out who did this awful thing." She kept her voice steady and calm, despite the emotions churning in her gut. "Now, if you don't mind, I have to work in the morning. Good night."

Linc stared at her for another long moment before turning toward the door. He got halfway when he abruptly stopped and glanced back over his shoulder. "If you didn't set the fire, you need to take some time to think about who did. Who could possibly be holding a grudge against you to do something as serious as this? While the fire turned out to be relatively harmless, the next time you may not be so fortunate. Another attempt could be far more deadly. You really need to consider who might be targeting you for some reason. Maybe someone you angered in the past."

Bands of fear tightened around her chest, making it difficult to breathe. Another attempt? She couldn't bear to think about it. "I'll try, but I'm not involved in a relationship and haven't been for eighteen months. I work as a physical therapy tech at the clinic in town. I highly doubt one of my patients hates me enough to do something like this." Although there were the occasional circumstances where patients had lashed out at her. Being in pain wasn't easy, as she knew all too well. She flexed her scarred fingers. Yet to go as far as to set a fire? No, she couldn't see it.

"Think harder," he said ominously before leaving through the front door.

Jayme drew in a deep, jagged breath as she went over to close and lock the door behind him. Then she slumped against the wood, sliding down until she was sitting with her back against the wall, her knees cradled up to her chest. She lowered her forehead to her knees and tried to quell the rising panic.

What was going on here? This whole thing didn't make any sense. A small fire set on purpose to send smoke into her house, but not enough to burn the place down? Who on earth would do something like that? And why?

As much as she desperately wanted to cling to her theory of neighborhood kids pulling some sort of prank, she couldn't deny there was a sinister tone to the vandalism. Granted, the fire had been contained, but what if it hadn't been? She had to think there was always the possibility it could have spiraled out of control.

Which left her with no choice but to accept Linc Quade's preposterous idea.

To think about who from her past was carrying a grudge

against her. Honestly, her first instinct would be to name the Preacher. Except he and his wife were dead. She and the other foster kids, Sawyer, Hailey, Darby, Cooper, Trent, and Caitlyn, had all hidden in the woods, watching and waiting for the adults to emerge from the fiery cabin.

They hadn't. And the way the cabin had burned so fast and so quickly, she felt certain there wouldn't have been time for the adults to get out. Especially since the Preacher had already been badly burned.

None of them had gone in to help rescue the Preacher or his wife either. A better person would have felt guilty about that, but she hadn't experienced an ounce of remorse. Not after the way he'd groped her, pinned her down with the intent to rape her. No, she hadn't gone in to rescue him.

By tacit agreement, she and the other foster kids had simply watched and waited.

When they heard the fire engines rushing toward the cabin, they finally began to move away, hiding deeper in the woods. They'd stayed together only briefly, long enough to agree that none of them were ever going back into the foster system.

To avoid being found, they'd split up and scattered. Sawyer, Cooper, and Trent had gone south. Hailey and Darby had gone due west, and she'd kept Caitlyn with her, heading in a northwest direction.

From that point on, she'd never seen her foster siblings again. Well, other than Caitlyn, whom she'd kept with her over the years, telling everyone the girl seven years her junior was her younger sister. To be honest, Jayme knew she'd mainly survived for Caitlyn's sake.

Sure, she could think about who might be carrying a grudge against her, maybe someone from the early days when she'd been forced to lie, cheat, and steal to stay alive. But that didn't seem at all likely.

And she highly doubted her old boyfriend Eli cared about what she was doing now. They'd parted amicably enough. He claimed she was standoffish, and he was probably right.

No, the simple answer was that this was either some sort of mistake, that someone had chosen her house instead of the one they'd really wanted.

But as she turned off the lights and tried to go back to sleep, she tossed and turned, her mind whirling.

She'd survived by trusting her instincts. And they were screaming at her now. Jayme knew, deep in her bones, the fire had been set on purpose to frighten her. And worse? Whoever had done it succeeded.

She was scared to death and had no idea what to do about it.

CHAPTER TWO

Linc Quade took another walk around the outside of Ms. Weston's house. Nothing had changed since he'd first arrived; he didn't find any additional clues to help him understand what had transpired here.

In his role as arson investigator, he covered Pigeon Forge, Gatlinburg, and Sevierville. If he hadn't lived in Sevierville, it would have taken him longer to get to Ms. Weston's house to see the scene of the fire. Well, actually, the concoction that had been created had been more of a homemade smoke bomb than an actual fire.

True arson cases were rare in this area. As the home-owner mentioned, kids often caused fires, but generally not on purpose. More because they made poor decisions. This close to the Smoky Mountains, most kids knew better than to let a fire get out of control. The Smoky Mountains weren't as dry as those forests on the West Coast, but they hadn't been blessed with much rain in the past ten days. Even a small campfire could do a fair amount of damage in a short time frame.

But this? Definitely set on purpose. And in such a way

that there was a very low possibility of causing the house to go up in flames. Which was not in character for most arsonists.

Firebugs, as they were called, loved to watch the dancing dragon in action. The bigger the fire, the better. And seeing their own masterpiece flare high and wide, devouring the structure surrounding it, was often what helped catch them. During his first major fire investigation, the guy who'd set the fire was discovered about a hundred feet away, gazing at the fire with such rapt fascination that he'd been easy to find and arrest. The traces of accelerant on his hands and clothes had linked him to the fire.

Not all arson fires were set by true arsonists. His most recent investigation had involved a fire set in order to get insurance money for the owner who had a failing business. Having been unable to sell the building, the old guy had tried to set it on fire in a way that wouldn't track back to him.

Linc had found and arrested the guy.

However, this strange concoction didn't have any of the usual characteristics of arson. The fact that it had been set in a way to produce more smoke than anything had made him wonder about the homeowner.

Ms. Jayme Weston's right hand had been badly burned in the past. That fact alone had moved her to the top of his suspect list.

Yet the flash of sheer terror in her eyes when he'd mentioned the fire had given him pause. No hint of fascination in those blue depths, only frank dread. Not to mention, she'd carried a baseball bat with her as a way to defend herself.

The situation was a puzzle, one he intended to get to the bottom of.

"Linc? Need anything else?" Ted Daniels, the fire-fighter who'd notified him of the possibility of arson, came over to join him. He and Ted had worked together and remained on friendly terms, in spite of the eight-year age gap between them.

"No, I'm good."

Ted glanced at the house. "Did she give you any idea who did this?"

"Not a hint. I left my card in case she comes up with a name." Linc shrugged and slapped Ted on the back. "Thanks again for the call."

"No problem." Ted turned and jumped up onto the back of the rig. Minutes later, they were on the road, heading back to the firehouse.

Linc watched them leave. A fire had cost him his family when he was twelve years old. He'd gotten out of the house, jumping from the second-story window, but his parents and his younger sister hadn't made it. Linc's Aunt Becca had taken him in. She and her husband, Flynn, were wonderful, and his young cousins had treated him like their older brother, never resenting his presence thrust upon them. But he'd never forgotten that day the fire had taken his family from him.

Of course, he'd become a firefighter. And then an arson investigator.

His goal had been to rescue people, to prevent the same thing that had happened to him. It was what he'd lived for, only he hadn't been able to help his wife and daughter, who'd been killed in a terrible multicar crash two years ago.

From that point forward, Linc knew he was meant to live alone. Sure, he'd sought solace in church, the way Aunt Becca had taught him, but he wasn't about to open his heart again.

To anyone.

Yet there was something about Ms. Weston that he found difficult to ignore. Maybe it was just the simple fact that she'd escaped a fire when she was young, much the way he had.

Or maybe he was just letting his hormones run amok.

Giving himself a mental shake, he walked toward his SUV. Time to head home and try to get some sleep. His report on the Weston fire could wait until morning.

But despite his best intentions, Linc mostly tossed and turned over the next few hours, finally dragging himself out of bed by five thirty. He made a pot of coffee and wrote up his report, shooting it to his boss and to the police department.

For a long moment, he stared at his computer screen. Curiosity got the better of him, so he set his coffee mug aside and did a basic search on Jayme Weston.

The first item to pop up was the physical therapy clinic where she worked. The website listed her as one of their staff members. She looked stunning in her photo, and he found it difficult to tear his gaze from her smiling face. Obviously, there had been nothing to smile about last night. In fact, she'd gotten angry with him.

He moved on but soon frowned. No social media. Who didn't do social media? Even he had a presence there, mostly to keep in touch with Aunt Becca and his cousins. He dug a little deeper, his access mirrored those in law enforcement, so he was able to pull up her driver's license.

But that was it. If he didn't know better, he'd think Jayme Weston was nothing more than a figment of his imagination.

Sitting back in his chair, he sipped more coffee. The woman lived alone, claimed to not be in a relationship, and worked as a physical therapy tech. Was she a loner by nature? What did she do for fun?

And who on earth had sent smoke into her house?

Linc was no closer to having answers as he began his day. He'd taken the homemade smoke bomb from the Weston fire to the lab, hoping to get something useful.

The lab tech had given him a doubtful look and told him not to hold his breath.

He had an office in the police station. It was an unusual setup, but he wasn't going to complain. His roots were firmly planted with his fellow firefighters, but investigating what had happened at the scene of the fire mirrored police work. His role straddled both departments.

After spending another hour trying to find other home-made smoke bombs that may have been set in the area, he eventually gave up. There was no indication of anyone doing something similar in the entire state of Tennessee or Kentucky.

The incident at the Weston house was unique. Which was both good and bad.

His phone rang, and he smiled when he saw Becca's name. "Hey, how are you?"

"Good, dear, how are you? Any chance you want to swing by for dinner? Your uncle Flynn is grilling steaks, and that could be a fire hazard."

He chuckled, even though this was an ongoing joke in the family. "Sure thing. Although you haven't invited any single women, right?"

"I promised I wouldn't," Becca said firmly. "Especially after you misbehaved last time."

Misbehaved? He hadn't done anything, which had really made her mad. As much as he loved his aunt, her attempt to fix him up with a woman had caused him to instantly turn away and leave without so much as saying goodbye. Afterward, he'd warned Becca to never try that again or he wouldn't attend any family gatherings.

She'd reluctantly agreed. But she hadn't apologized, claiming he needed to move on with his life.

"Okay, then. I should be able to come, unless a call comes in."

"Great, we'll see you around six. Take care and don't work too hard." Becca disconnected from the line. He shook his head at her unwavering love and support. Even in those years when he'd rebelled, badly, she'd stuck by him.

He wouldn't be the man he was today without her.

But no matter what she said, he wasn't going to open his heart again. He was happy with his life just as it was.

Linc took his usual hour-long break at lunchtime to head to the gym. Lifting weights, punching the bag, and generally sweating his socks off helped him to cope after losing Gina and Melody. Now it was so much a part of his routine, he couldn't imagine going through a day without a stiff workout.

Normally, the intense physical exertion kept him from thinking too much about what he'd lost. Almost as if the sweat running in streams off his body was like shedding tears. Letting go of the past hurts, and the pain. He always came out of a workout feeling refreshed.

Today, though, working out didn't help keep him focused. For some odd reason, no matter how hard he punched the bag, he couldn't seem to pry the image of Jayme Weston out of his mind.

Frankly, he didn't like it. The woman had no business interrupting his workout. Impinging on his thoughts. After he'd showered and changed, he'd had to force himself not to head over to the physical therapy clinic where she worked under the pretense of asking follow-up questions.

He didn't have any follow-up questions. Not unless she'd come up with a possible suspect. And he'd given her his card, so she could call him if she had.

She hadn't. So that was that.

Thankfully, he had a meeting with the fire and police commissioner that afternoon. At this point, he'd welcome any distraction to keep him from thinking of his latest arson victim.

JAYME FINISHED WORKING with Mrs. Jackson, a sweet sixty-five-year-old woman who was still recovering from her total knee replacement surgery that had been done three weeks ago. "You're doing great, Mrs. Jackson."

"Thank you, Miss Jayme." Here in the south, people clung to their manners. "I only have two more visits that have been approved by my insurance. Do you think that's enough?"

Insurance companies were the bane of healthcare, especially those in physical therapy. "The physical therapist will try to file an appeal, but regardless, you really need to keep doing the home exercises I gave you." Jayme could tell the sweet lady wasn't doing them on a daily basis as recommended. "That's the best way for you to recover full range of motion."

"Okay, I promise." Mrs. Jackson leaned on her cane as she left the gym.

All day, Jayme had been looking at her patients through jaded lenses. Despite her best intentions, she'd tried to imagine any of them being angry or upset enough to track down where she lived and start a small fire.

Most of her patients were either elderly like Mrs. Jackson or young athletes who'd been injured playing sports. There weren't many in between.

Her last patient of the day was a young man named Gary Albrecht. When he came into the clinic, he wore his usual scowl. The kid had suffered a bad knee injury playing football, and it appeared his playing days were over.

Only he hadn't been ready to admit it.

"Hi, Gary. How are you feeling?" She pasted a smile on her face.

"Like crap. My knee still hurts like crazy." He limped over and took a seat on the stationary bike to do his five minutes of warm-up exercises, knowing the routine well enough that he didn't need to be told. "You need to do something to convince that stupid surgeon to give me more pain meds."

"I'll make a note in your chart," Jayme said, grateful that she didn't have the power to prescribe narcotics.

"Won't help," Gary snapped irritably. "Doc is a masochist. Claims I shouldn't need them anymore." He cursed under his breath.

Of all her patients today, Gary was the only one who wasn't grateful for the services she provided. Yet even with his permanent scowl and simmering anger, she couldn't imagine him sneaking out to her house to set a fire.

Now if the doc who was refusing to prescribe the pain meds was the victim, maybe. But even then, Gary didn't look like an arsonist.

Not that she had any clue what an arsonist should look like.

"I know it's painful but do your best." This was one

environment where her scarred hand worked in her favor. It helped her patients know she understood what they were going through as she'd suffered a similar fate.

She guided Gary through his exercises, trying to ignore his cranky attitude. When he cursed again, though, she glared at him.

"Stop it! You know full well that sort of language will get you discharged from care." The clinic had a policy of not tolerating abusive behavior; the large poster on the wall helped to reinforce the message. "Are you here to get better or not?"

"Not," Gary shot back. And to her surprise, he turned and limped away. "I'm done with you and this place."

Battling a wave of guilt, she stared after his retreating figure. Sandra Jones, one of the physical therapist's she worked for, came over. "What was that about?"

"He kept swearing, so I told him to stop it or he'd be discharged from care." Jayme sighed. "Unfortunately, he discharged himself."

"Was he still going on about the pain meds?" Sandra asked.

Jayme nodded. "Yeah. I'm worried he'll find a way to get what he needs without a doctor's order."

Substance abuse and the opioid epidemic were nothing new. Living on the streets with Caitlyn had given her a front-row view of those who chose to abuse drugs. They weren't hard to find, she'd watched many a drug deal go down in the past. And somehow she suspected Gary was heading down a dark and dangerous path.

Sandra sighed. "We can only do our best."

"I know. Still, I probably could have handled that better."

"You're not responsible for his actions," Sandra said firmly. "He is."

Jayme nodded. Being responsible for your own actions was the mantra she'd lived by since running away from the Preacher's cabin. Jayme knew full well she couldn't stop Gary from doing whatever he wanted. Even if that meant buying illegal drugs.

Over the past thirteen years, she'd done everything possible to keep Caitlyn fed, sheltered, and protected from predators. It had been her sole mission in life.

And she'd succeeded. Mostly through hard work but also with an unexpected boon from a seventy-year-old man named Remy Edgar.

Remy was gone now, died of a heart attack six years ago. She missed him; he'd been the only parental figure in her life. Or rather, the only one she'd looked up to. Certainly not her drug-addicted and prostitute mother who'd tried selling Jayme to one of her pimps, or her jailed-for-murder father. No, Remy was the real deal. She'd been his waitress at the local café when her scarred hand had caught his attention. As a retired physical therapist, he'd expressed concern for the lack of treatment she'd received for her burn and had taught her various hand exercises she needed to do in order to improve her range of motion.

She'd lied about her age, of course, in order to get the café job. She suspected Remy knew, but he'd never ratted her out. During that time, she and Caitlyn lived in a horrible trailer home that she could barely afford. But it was better than the seedy motel where she'd had to fight predators off on a daily basis.

Remy must have realized how desperate she was because slowly, over time, he'd begun to help her out in a variety of other ways. Not just leaving ridiculously large tips, but often bringing her food he claimed he couldn't eat and would go to waste if she didn't take it. At first, she'd been leery of his attention, keeping him at arm's length. Her second motto during those years had been to trust no one. But Remy had persisted, eventually showing her a picture of his daughter and granddaughter, saying she reminded him of his family.

One day he'd asked her to stop by his house, claiming he had more food to give her. Again, she'd almost refused, fearing this was nothing more than an elaborate trap to get her alone and to attack. She rode her bicycle, the only method of transportation she owned—and a stolen one at that—back and forth in front of his house before going up the driveway, hoping plenty of people would notice her if she ended up going missing.

Remy had surprised her by showing her a small apartment over the garage. Far enough from the house to provide privacy, along with an outdoor set of stairs leading into the place, and a brand-new dead bolt lock on the door. When he'd suggested she and Caitlyn move in, she'd thrown his offer back in his face, telling him she wasn't going to pay him rent by sleeping with him. The poor man had looked truly horrified by her allegation. She soon learned that what Remy really wanted was a helping hand with the cleaning and laundry. He'd told her how his wife had died shortly before they'd met and that he couldn't cook without burning the house down. Remy convinced her that he truly just wanted to help. By cleaning his house one day a week and doing his laundry, he allowed her and Caitlyn to live in the garage apartment rent-free.

A deal too good to pass up.

She'd learned to trust Remy and his kind generosity. Even though they'd had to share the single bedroom, the garage apartment was so much nicer than the trailer that she'd pinched herself each morning to make sure it wasn't a dream. For the first time ever, she'd been able to actually save some money after buying groceries and other necessities.

Unfortunately, they'd only had four years of living with Remy. One day he'd suffered a massive heart attack while she'd been at work at the café and Caitlyn had been at school. To her horror, he'd been pronounced dead in the emergency department.

Losing Remy was devastating, and only then did she realize how much she'd come to care for him. How much she'd miss him now that he was gone. Yet she was even more shocked to discover Remy had provided her and Caitlyn a small dowry in his will. Ten thousand dollars with a note begging her to use the money toward attending college.

Remy's grandkids, Gloria and Marco, had flown in from California to take over selling the house. Marco had been upset at learning about the ten grand, and she'd nearly given it back. If not for needing that money to ensure Caitlyn's welfare, she would have walked away. After the argument, Marco had left in a huff, and she'd never seen him again.

Jayme glanced around the now empty clinic, knowing her job here today was the result of Remy's kindness. His unselfish generosity in helping a couple of runaway foster kids. Granted, she'd done her fair share, holding two jobs to make ends meet while taking classes. She hadn't wanted to spend all Remy's money, in fact, she'd pretty much hoarded it while supporting Caitlyn through high school and then on to college. She'd used part of Remy's money as a down payment for the house. Caitlyn was almost finished with her associate degree as a veterinary tech, the only career she'd consider because of how much she loved animals.

When Caitlyn graduated this December, Jayme could be satisfied in knowing that Remy's modest endowment meant they'd both graduated in their chosen fields with four years of college credit between them along with a roof over their heads.

Not bad for two foster kids with fake names and IDs. There wasn't a single doubt in her mind that without Remy, she'd still be living in that awful trailer and working as a waitress.

Caitlyn too.

Jayme pulled herself together and focused on finishing her notes on Gary's visit. As diplomatically as possible, she'd outlined his concern over pain management, his foul language, and his walking out in the middle of his appointment. When that was finished, she helped put the equipment away. The clinic closed early on Fridays, her day ending at four o'clock, which was nice. Especially today. She was physically and mentally exhausted, having been unable to fall back to sleep last night after the fire.

Lincoln Quade's business card was burning a hole in her pocket. Several times she'd had to prevent herself from pulling it out to look at it.

As if the small white card held the answers to her questions.

"Have any plans this weekend?" Sandra asked as they met in the small locker room.

Jayme shrugged as she opened her locker and removed her purse and jacket. "Not really. The usual."

"Girl, you need to forget about that jerk and find yourself a new man," Sandra said with a wide grin.

To her shame, Linc's face popped into her mind. She ruthlessly shoved it away. "Nah, I don't need a man. They're more trouble than they're worth."

"Not the right man," Sandra countered.

"Hey, you scooped up the only good guy in town." Sandra's fiancé, George, was a sweetheart, and the two of them were perfect for each other. She slammed her locker. "Have a good one."

"You too, hon," Sandra called to her retreating figure.

Jayme didn't dare mention that the highlight of her weekend would be to volunteer at the food pantry for five hours on Saturday morning. A job she did every weekend. Not that she was ashamed of doing the work, but she knew Sandra would try to convince her to go out with one of George's friends. Personally, she'd rather be at the food pantry than go out on another blind date. After Remy's kindness, she'd felt the need to give back in some way.

By some standards, her five hours might not seem like much, but Irene Lambert, the woman who ran the pantry, insisted that every little bit helped.

And now that Caitlyn had moved out, she had more time on her hands than usual.

Slipping her purse strap over her shoulder, Jayme walked toward her car. She paused when she heard the sound of music playing and almost turned and headed toward the pub. Music was something she loved, but sitting in a crowded room with strangers? Not so much.

She liked her patients, but those visits were short and focused on regaining health and mobility. Each patient came with a goal that they either met or made some sort of progress toward.

Idle chitchat wasn't her forte.

And a single woman in a pub on a Friday afternoon would draw men the way a neon sign drew gnats.

Ugh. Who needed the headache?

Still, she leaned against her car for a moment, listening

to the country-western music drifting from the outdoor patio. It was difficult to admit that Sandra might be right. Ever since Caitlyn had moved out, she'd felt at loose ends. Jayme had been the one to encourage Caitlyn to move on with her life. To experience all those things Jayme hadn't been able to.

She was proud of the young woman her foster sister had become.

Even if she missed Caitlyn like crazy.

Don't you think it's time to stop feeling sorry for yourself? Her inner critic didn't pull any punches.

She pushed away from the car and opened the driver's side door. She was a twenty-nine-year-old woman experiencing empty-nest syndrome.

The pathetic thought brought a reluctant smile. Good grief. How sad was that?

Honestly, she needed to get a grip. Just because her life had been focused for so long on Caitlyn didn't mean she had nothing else to offer. Remy would be extremely upset to know she was wallowing in this sort of self-pity. She was young, there were plenty of things she could do, important things. She had her writing, but she viewed it as a hobby more than anything. She could possibly go back to school to become a real physical therapist. She was smart, and the clinic would likely provide her a good reference.

Time to pull herself together. After tossing her purse into the passenger seat, she slid behind the wheel of her ancient Ford Fiesta. It had over a hundred and twenty thousand miles on it, but so far, it was holding up. And it was better than using the stolen bicycle. Thankfully, she only drove around town, not trusting the vehicle to get her to Nashville or anywhere else for that matter.

The last stanza of the country-western song drifted

toward her. With a wry smile, she cranked the key in the ignition.

The car started up without a problem, but before she could put the vehicle into drive, the hood of her car burst open with a loud pop, and she gasped when the engine went up in flames.

What in the world? Jayme frantically pushed out of the car, making a quick grab for her purse before running away from the burning vehicle as fast as possible. She'd made it several blocks before she heard the loud *boom*.

She swung around, looking back at her old Fiesta with horror. Billows of black smoke surrounded the car, and even from that distance, she could see the flicker of yellow and orange.

Fire. Her car was on fire.

Her knees threatened to buckle beneath her weight. First the smoke in her house and now a car fire.

Who had done this?

And what was coming next?

CHAPTER THREE

Linc was heading home to change for dinner with his aunt Becca when the call came in. He winced, knowing she'd be upset if he couldn't attend the family gathering. "Yeah?"

"You've been requested to go to the scene of a car fire," the dispatcher informed him.

"Car fires aren't usually arson," he pointed out.

"Car belongs to a Ms. Jayme Weston. She requested you specifically, asked if you could please respond ASAP."

Relief washed over him knowing Jayme was okay enough to have made the call. Then he went tense. "Where is she?"

The dispatcher rattled off the information, but he was already stomping on the brake to execute a tight U-turn. He should have guessed her car was still at the physical therapy clinic where Jayme worked.

Was it possible the fire was a result of her car overheating? Not likely. Two fires in less than twenty-four hours were not a coincidence. It was clear Jayme was being targeted by this particular nontraditional firebug.

And if he believed what she'd told him, she had no idea who would do such a thing.

Linc sent up a silent prayer for God to keep Jayme safe. Considering she'd asked for him, he felt certain she must not be badly hurt. Yet she may have sustained minor burns.

The image of her scarred hand flashed in his mind, but he thrust it away impatiently.

He knew firebugs. Knew how they thought, how they worked. They didn't target people like this. Normally, they searched for easy prey, like old dilapidated buildings that would go up in a beautiful flash of fiery orange and yellow flames. Barns with lots of dried hay were a particular favorite.

Arson car fires were mostly used to cover up evidence of a crime. But he didn't think that was the motive here.

No, he knew this car fire was a specific warning for Jayme herself. One she couldn't afford to ignore.

He pulled up in front of the clinic five minutes later. Jayme was standing off to the side wearing a pair of blue scrubs covered by a dark blue jacket. When she saw him, he caught a flash of relief cross her features.

"You're not hurt?" he asked tersely even as he raked his gaze over her, searching for any signs of injury.

She shook her head. Her red hair was loose around her shoulders. "I was able to get away." Her husky voice trembled in a way that made him long to pull her into his arms.

He pushed away the inappropriate thought. "What happened?"

"I—just turned on the car." Her blue gaze appeared bewildered. "There was a loud sound, and the hood popped open. When I saw flames shooting out, I bailed from the car and ran."

He glanced over to her bright yellow Ford Fiesta. The

damage was centered on the engine; the rest of the car appeared untouched. The Fiesta was an older model, Ford didn't even make them anymore, making it possible this could have been the result of an engine malfunction. Still, he wasn't buying the coincidence. "Stay here, I need to check it out."

"Okay." She hugged herself despite the mild temperatures. Belatedly realizing she was vulnerable out there, he changed his mind and reached out to lightly grasp her arm. If the firebug was out there watching, he wanted to keep her close.

"Better that you stick with me." He drew her toward her not so sunny car. The firefighter crew was different from the guys who'd responded last night. They worked twenty-four hours on and forty-eight hours off. Sometimes the twenty-four hours on dragged on long and boring. But not today.

"Meyers, what do you have?" He addressed the senior member of the group of firefighters.

"Hey, Linc." Meyers gestured toward the Fiesta. "Incendiary device apparently rigged to start on fire with added gunpowder to make a small bomb. At least from what we can tell." Meyers grinned. "That part is up to you."

"Yeah." Linc stared at the charred remains sitting on top of the vehicle's engine. It was an odd way to get someone's attention. Why start a fire, then cause an explosion? It didn't make any sense. He turned toward Jayme. "And you're sure you didn't accidentally pop the hood by hitting the latch?"

"Positive."

He nodded and drew her away from the Fiesta. The fire was out, but the car was too hot for him to learn anything more. He'd need to wait until it cooled down to begin his formal investigation. "I'm glad you called to ask for my help. Do you have somewhere to stay tonight?"

"You mean other than my house?" She shivered and shook her head. "No. But I'll be fine."

"This isn't something to take lightly." His tone came out harsher than he intended, and he did his best to soften it. "Ms. Weston, I'm worried about you. I suggest you stay the night with a friend."

She stared at him for a long moment. "What about my car?"

"It will be towed to the police garage. I'll need to examine the device that started the fire more closely."

"Do you plan to compare this one to what you found outside my house?"

"Basically, yes." Although he already knew the two devices were very different. One was made to cause smoke, the other to cause a fire. There were components, like phosphates and other chemicals, that may be similar. But he didn't want her to get caught up in the details. "I'll give you a ride to a friend's house."

She grimaced as she glanced around at the firefighters who were already packing up to leave. "I guess I can go to a motel, but I'd like to stop at home first. Pick up a few things."

A motel? He didn't know why her decision bothered him, but it did. He wanted to ask why she'd ruled out going to a friend's place. She worked in the clinic, surely someone there would be willing to help her out.

Linc bit his tongue to stop from asking a slew of questions, none of which were his business. "Fine, I'll take you home, then drop you off at a motel. Which one?"

"The Shady Lane Motel."

He winced before he could stop himself. "Really? It's not a nice place."

She shrugged and avoided his gaze. "It's cheap."

He didn't doubt the place was cheap, not that he'd ever been there. But he was curious as to how she knew the room rates. Had she stayed there in the past? Honestly, it didn't seem like her type of place.

Then again, Linc knew next to nothing about her, so maybe it was her type of place. He reminded himself that her past was none of his concern, despite the fact that he was insatiably curious about her.

"Linc? You need anything else?" Meyers asked.

"You've arranged for this to be taken to the police garage?" When Meyers nodded, he smiled. "I'm good, then. Thanks."

"See you." Meyers glanced curiously at Jayme before returning to the fire rig.

"My vehicle is this way, Ms. Weston," he said, gesturing toward his black SUV.

"Jayme." She fell into step beside him. She let out a weary sigh. "You may as well call me Jayme."

"Okay, Jayme. I'm Linc." He glanced at her. "I gave you my card, why didn't you call me directly?"

"The car was on fire, and I wasn't sure if the gas tank would explode, so I called the emergency operator." A hint of a smile tugged at the corner of her mouth. "Never called 911 in my life until today. Twice in twenty-four hours must be a new record."

"Most cars don't explode the way you see on TV, but I can understand your concern. I'm sorry you had to go through that." He opened the passenger door for her. She looked surprised but then climbed in. "I'm sure it was frightening."

"Yeah." All humor faded from her face. "I'm worried, Linc. This person has struck out at me twice in twenty-four hours. What is he planning next?"

"I wish I knew." He hated knowing she had every right to be concerned. He closed her door and rounded the vehicle. He took a moment to text his aunt Becca an apology about missing dinner due to a call, then climbed in behind the wheel. Moments later, he had the SUV on the road heading toward her house.

"I had a patient today who got pretty upset," she said, breaking the silence.

He arched a brow. "Did he threaten you?"

"No. He was swearing at me, and when I reminded him about our policy against foul language, he stormed out." She glanced at him. "He was upset with his surgeon not renewing his pain meds."

He could understand how a patient may take that type of frustration out on a therapist. "Did he think you were responsible for the surgeon's decision?"

"No." She waved a hand. "This is what I'm trying to tell you. My patients might get angry or upset, but there's really no reason for one of them to do something like this."

"I agree, it's a stretch." He turned the wheel to enter her driveway. "And you're absolutely sure there isn't anyone else who could be holding a grudge against you?"

She hesitated for a long moment. "There is one possibility, but it's a very remote one. Will probably turn out to be nothing."

His pulse kicked up. "Who?"

"A man named Marco Edgar." She pushed open her door. "It's a long story. I can fill you in on the details later. But I wanted you to have his name so you can cross him off the list."

"Hold on, I'm going in with you." He quickly joined her as she walked up the driveway. "Give me your key, I'll go in first."

To her credit, Jayme didn't argue. She handed him her house key and then stood back as he entered the building, looking for any sign of an intruder. Jayme stayed to his back as he cleared one room and the other, verifying the place was empty.

"Grab your things."

"Thanks." She disappeared into the bedroom.

Linc stood in the middle of the living room, his thoughts whirling. The fact that this guy had struck while her car was at the clinic meant he knew her schedule. Knew when she worked, when she was home.

This Marco guy she'd mentioned? The name didn't mean anything to him, but Sevierville wasn't that small. He'd grown up here in town but had also worked in Knoxville for several years. He certainly didn't know everyone in the area.

He made a mental note to run the name past his aunt Becca, after he apologized again for missing dinner.

"I'm ready." Jayme had changed into soft, comfortable blue jeans and a dark green sweater. She had a duffel bag looped over her shoulder.

He took the bag from her and escorted her back outside. Before he could talk himself out of it, he asked, "Are you hungry?"

"Why?"

"You said you had a long story to tell, and we both need to eat." He glanced at her. "There's a nice Italian place not far from here."

"I—uh, sure. Why not." She looked flustered by his offer. He could relate.

Linc told himself that he needed to hear more about Marco Edgar, but somehow, taking Jayme to his favorite Italian restaurant felt like a date.

THE MORE JAYME thought about her situation, it seemed highly unlikely that Marco was running around Sevierville starting fires to scare her.

But honestly, he was the only person she could think of that might be holding a grudge against her.

She'd briefly considered her foster siblings but then dismissed the notion. They'd all hated the Preacher, had been grateful to escape the burning cabin.

Had all vowed to never go back into foster care ever again.

No, it didn't make sense. None of it made sense.

Yet the two incidents had been all too real.

As Linc pulled into the crowded parking lot of Della Maria's, she remembered it was a Friday night. "We don't have a reservation."

"I don't think we'll need one." He shrugged and added, "I know the owner."

No surprise there. She swallowed a sigh. Linc was the kind of guy who made friends easily and likely knew everyone in town.

As different from her as a bear to a mouse.

And she was the mouse.

True to his word, when they entered the restaurant, a woman came rushing over to greet him. "Lincoln, it's been too long. Oh, and you brought a lovely guest." The woman's keen eyes swept over Jayme, not missing a thing.

"Della Maria, this is Jayme Weston. Jayme, Maria is the

owner and a friend of my aunt Becca."

"What he means is we are family." Maria beamed. "Come, I have the perfect table for you in the corner." The woman's personality was larger than life, and Jayme nearly choked when she winked at her, as if in approval of a personal relationship developing between them, before leading the way through the restaurant to a secluded table in the corner. "I hope this works for you?"

"Absolutely, thanks, Maria." Linc gathered the older woman in for a hug and a kiss on the cheek. "You're the best."

"Of course I am." Maria patted his cheek. "Anything for you, Lincoln. Enjoy your evening." Maria quickly moved away, chatting with other guests as she returned to the front of the restaurant.

"Wow, she's—something," Jayme said as she sank into the seat across from Linc. "I'm surprised she's the owner and not the chef."

"Her husband, Dimitri, is the chef." He eyed her across the table. "Sorry if she made it sound as if this was a date."

"It's fine." She fell silent as a server filled their water glasses. When they were alone again, she reached for the menu. "You'll have to tell me what's good."

"It's all great," he said with a chuckle. "But the chicken marsala is one of my favorites."

The prices seemed awfully high, then again, she didn't dine out in places like this. The price for the spaghetti and meatballs seemed reasonable, so she decided to go with that.

After they'd placed their order, Linc leaned forward. "Tell me about this Marco guy."

She quickly explained about Remy Edgar and the money he'd left her and Caitlyn six years ago. She ended the story with how upset Remy's grandson had been at learning about the money his grandfather had given them. "I told you it was a long shot, but he's the only person I could think of who might be holding a grudge against me."

"Back up, Jayme. Who is Caitlyn?"

"My younger sister. She recently moved out with a friend who is also finishing up her veterinary tech program. They work together too."

"Why didn't you mention a sister last night?" Linc asked.

"Because she's not involved in this."

"Except this Remy guy left you both the money, right?"

She frowned, wondering why he was so focused on this aspect of the story. "Yes, but Caitlyn was a minor then. I'm the one who handled the inheritance. I used some for my schooling, for hers, and for the house."

"Impressive."

She couldn't tell if he was being serious or simply humoring her. "I know ten grand isn't a lot of money by most people's standards, but it was life changing for us." She didn't add that Remy's grandson, Marco, had shown up wearing top of the line clothes and a Rolex watch.

Once she'd have tried to take it from him.

But she gave up stealing a long time ago.

"Did you lose your parents in the fire?"

His question jolted her enough that she spilled some of her water. "No. Why would you ask that?"

"Because you haven't been entirely forthcoming with me, have you?" His dark gaze bored into hers.

She took a long sip of her water in an effort to get her emotions under control. "I grew up in the foster system. My mother was a prostitute and drug addict, my father is serving life in prison for murder. I guarantee neither of them are involved in this."

His gaze flashed with remorse. "I'm sorry to hear that, but maybe someone is trying to get to you as a way of punishing your father."

"After all this time?" She shook her head. "Doubtful. I barely remember him, he was gone by my fifth birthday. That was twenty-four years ago."

"Caitlyn must have been an infant."

She averted her gaze, glancing around the crowded restaurant. The arson investigator was far too detail-focused for her peace of mind. No doubt an admirable quality when it came to his work.

But she didn't appreciate people prying into her personal life. Especially the life before she'd escaped from the Preacher. No one needed to know she and Caitlyn weren't related by blood. They'd lived as sisters for the past thirteen years, and that was all that mattered. "Caitlyn is seven years younger than me. We're foster siblings, not related by blood."

"Okay, could someone from one of the foster homes be involved?"

The image of the Preacher screaming in agony as he clawed at the oil burning his face flashed in her mind. It took every ounce of willpower she had not to react. "No. There was one difficult home, but those people died a long time ago."

His uncanny glance dropped to her burned hand, and she battled a wave of anxiety. She felt certain she wasn't fooling Lincoln Quade one bit.

She was barely fooling herself.

"My last foster family was thirteen years ago. The night of the fire, a man who called himself the Preacher tried to rape me. So yes, I threw the lantern at him and started a fire. But we escaped, and he and his wife didn't." She glared at him. "Happy now? You know the entire sordid painful truth. But none of that is going to help us find the person responsible for"—she waved a hand—"I don't know, arson stalking me."

His jaw dropped. "Look, Jayme, I'm sorry—"

"Don't." She cut him off. "It doesn't matter. I left my past behind a long time ago. I've come a long way since then, and I'm doing fine. At least I was until last night. Can we please just focus on the fires?"

Linc didn't have a chance to respond because their server brought over their meals. Linc had gone with his favorite, but she personally thought her spaghetti and meat-balls looked much more appealing.

Although just thinking about the years she and the other fosters had spent living with the Preacher was enough to steal her appetite.

Linc bowed his head for a moment before meeting her gaze and reaching for his fork. She'd never shared a meal with someone who prayed before eating, and she was slightly annoyed that Linc had once again knocked her off-kilter.

The man was more complicated than a Rubik's Cube.

And she'd never been able to figure out that puzzle.

Avoiding his gaze, she dug into her meal. As soon as she tasted the tangy sauce, her appetite returned with a vengeance. "This is incredible."

Linc grinned. "Told you."

She tried to eat slowly, to savor the food. Having learned to cook through necessity, she was no novice in the kitchen, but this? It made her wonder if Dimitri and Della Maria had brought over some secret sauce straight from Italy.

On cue, Della Maria sashayed over. "How is your meal tonight? Excellent, yes?"

"Yes!" There was no point in denying her exuberance. "Best ever, thank you so much."

"Ah, you are so sweet." Della Maria bent to place her arm around her shoulders and looked at Linc. "I like her, Linc. She's a keeper."

"Oh, uh . . ." She tried to think of a way to correct Della Maria's assumption.

"I'm aware," Linc said dryly. "Please let Dimitri know how much we are enjoying his food."

"Of course. Take care, Linc. Jayme." Della Maria patted her shoulder. "Don't be a stranger, come back anytime."

"Thank you." She wasn't about to promise to return since dining at restaurants as nice as this were outside her limited budget. But if she had more money, she'd definitely come back here.

Better not to go down that twisty path of wanting what you couldn't have. The food was so good she'd almost forgotten the only reason she was here with Linc in the first place was because some weirdo arsonist had caused her house to fill with smoke and then had set her car on fire.

Jayme forced herself to save half her meal for the next day. Linc asked for a to-go box, then paid the bill.

"Ready?" He slowly rose to his feet.

"Yes, thanks. That was great." She made sure to take her leftovers as she followed him through the restaurant and outside to his SUV.

Once again, he opened the car door for her, and she realized that no one, not even the sweet Remy, had ever done that for her. "Should I apologize?" His low, husky voice made her shiver.

"For what?" It was impossible to think clearly when he

was so close. She quickly slid into the seat, resting her to-go box on her lap.

"Della Maria and my aunt Becca have been trying to set me up for the past year. I'm sorry you were caught in the crosshairs tonight."

If there was ever a man who didn't need to be set up, it was the handsome, dark-eyed arson investigator. "Why on earth would they do that?"

He glanced away. "My wife and daughter died two years ago. They think it's time for me to move on with my life."

Open mouth and insert foot. "I'm so sorry." The words sounded inadequate. "I shouldn't have asked, it's just . . ." She couldn't think of a tactful explanation. "I'm sure their efforts come from a place of kindness."

He sighed. "I'm not sure about that at all, but I just wanted to explain why Maria pounced on you like that. She's normally more—subtle."

A choked laugh erupted before she could stop it. Subtle was not the word she would have used to describe Della Maria, but she wisely kept her thoughts to herself. Linc smiled ruefully, closed her door, then went around to climb in behind the wheel.

Time to change the subject. "Do you know where the Shady Lane Motel is located?"

His features tightened into a frown, but he nodded. "Yeah." He started the car and threw the gear shift into reverse. "I'd rather take you someplace else."

"I'll be fine." Paying for a motel went against the grain, but no way was she going to risk putting Caitlyn and her friend Annette in danger by heading over to their two-bedroom apartment.

"What about your sister?" Linc asked. "Is she okay?"

"I called her this morning before work. She's fine." Jayme knew the apartment was in Annette's name, which in hindsight was a good thing. "She promised to check in with me if she sees anything out of the ordinary."

"How long ago did she move out?" Linc asked.

"Just last month." She abruptly straightened. "Do you think this guy setting the fires isn't aware of that? Maybe he thinks she's still living with me?"

"The way he torched your car makes me think you're the target, not Caitlyn." He glanced at her, then added, "But I'm glad you warned her about the danger."

"Me too." She eased back against the seat cushion. "Better me be the target than her."

Linc drove for a while in silence. The Shady Lane Motel was on the outskirts of town and looked even worse than she remembered. She hid her reaction as Linc slowed down to take the turn.

Then he suddenly straightened the vehicle and hit the gas.

"What are you doing?" She frowned when they drove past the motel. "You missed the turn."

"I'm not dropping you off there." Linc's jaw flexed. "It's a crime scene waiting to happen."

"Look, I appreciate your concern, but—"

"You're staying at my place, end of discussion."

"No, I'm not." She grabbed the handle of the car. "And if you don't turn around right now, I'll jump out of the car."

"What?" He looked at her in shock. "I'm just trying to help you out."

Without warning, she released her seat belt and opened the car door. Linc hit the brakes, coming to a jarring halt. She grabbed her bag, jumped from the car, and ran as if the devil himself was coming after her.

CHAPTER FOUR

What had just happened?

Linc didn't understand, but no way was he letting her stay in that roach-infested motel. The very thought was repugnant. He quickly executed a tight turn and drove up alongside her running figure.

Jayme was fast, he'd give her that. When she reached the motel, he quickly parked and jumped from the car.

"Jayme, can we please talk about this?" He held up his hands in a gesture of surrender. "I'm sorry if I came off as dictatorial, but this place is awful. Please don't stay here."

"I'm not coming to your place." She tipped her chin defiantly. "If you're thinking I'm going to pay you for your kindness in the sack, you're dead wrong."

"No!" He mentally kicked himself for not realizing where her mind had gone. "Never. I would never ask that of you." Yet someone must have for that knee-jerk reaction to his suggestion. "I'm sorry." He glanced at the dilapidated building. "I'll take you to another hotel. A nicer one. One that doesn't have more roaches than people."

"I'm not made of money," she snapped. In the dim light,

he could see her cheeks were flushed. From the run or because of the assumption she'd made?

Probably both.

"I'll pay."

"That's not the point. I can afford it, but I don't know how long I'll have to be here." Jayme had calmed down a bit, providing a more constructive conversation. "This place rents rooms by the week."

Again, he didn't even want to think about how she knew that. "Please, Jayme. If you stay here, I'll be sleeping in my car parked outside your door."

"I can't control what you do." She adjusted the strap of her duffel. "I'll be fine. Just go do your job and find this guy."

Linc stared at her, trying to come up with a way to change her mind. A door opened, revealing a drunk man who stumbled from one of the rooms. The door slammed behind him, but his gaze had already locked on Jayme.

"Hey, pretty lady," he greeted her with a leer and a drunken slur. "How much?"

Jayme sighed. Before he could head over to tell the guy off, she swung her duffel so that it hit the drunk man square in the chest. He was so surprised and unstable he went sailing backward, landing hard on the asphalt. "Get lost," she told him. Then she turned toward Linc. "Fine, we can go somewhere else."

The way she'd handled herself made him grin. "You're good," he said approvingly.

"Lots of practice," she muttered wryly.

A mixture of horror and relief washed over him as she returned to his SUV. It must have been a rough time in her life that she'd been forced to stay here. He slid behind the wheel and drove away, ignoring the drunken man who'd managed to get back on his feet long enough to shout curses at them.

Linc glanced at Jayme. "Let me start again. I'm not interested in taking advantage of you. I'm not looking for anything other than friendship. Losing my wife and daughter left a hole in my heart that cannot be repaired. When I suggested you stay at my house, I meant in the guest bedroom. With your own bathroom and plenty of privacy."

"You didn't suggest, you demanded."

"I know. I'm sorry." He shouldn't have let his emotions get the better of him. "But the thought of you staying in that place made me sick to my stomach."

"It's not exactly my favorite place to stay." She bent down to pick up the leftovers that had fallen to the floor.

Then why on earth had she chosen it? Just because it was cheap? Her house was small, but it was neat and well kept. She didn't come across as barely making ends meet.

Then again, he wasn't privy to her financial situation.

"Jayme, I will find this guy who's targeted you, but I'll also sleep better knowing you're safe. You can choose where to spend the night—my place or a nicer hotel." Oddly enough, he was secretly hoping she'd pick his place.

"Where do you live?"

Inside, he executed a fist pump. "Not far from the city hall and police station."

"Fine." She glared at him. "I hope the spare bedroom door has a lock."

"It does." It saddened him that she felt she needed one. Then again, look at what had just happened at the Shady Lane? For all he knew, that was a common occurrence. "Thank you."

She let out a rusty laugh. "That's supposed to be my

line."

He hated knowing he'd scared her into running. "I can't lie, I'm insulted you thought I was the kind of guy who would ask for that kind of payment. I hope you know you can trust me."

Jayme didn't say anything for a long moment. "I guess I shouldn't have jumped to conclusions. It's just—most men want something. They might pretty it up with flowers and dinner, but at the end of the day, they still all want the same thing."

"Not all men." Again, he was horrified by her experiences. "But clearly, I've never been in your shoes."

"No, you haven't." She managed a tight smile. "I—uh, don't actually have a lot of close friends. I'm a bit rusty at this sort of thing."

He wanted to ask why she didn't have friends but held back. Now that he'd convinced her to stay at his place, he was reluctant to push her out of her comfort zone. "That's fine with me. We'll figure it out as we go."

She nodded and fell silent. The ride to his house didn't take long, and she eyed it curiously as he pulled into the garage. "Nice place."

"Thanks." He'd sold the house his wife had picked out to get something smaller. One that didn't have so many memories associated with it. He stopped in the kitchen and gestured to the fridge. "You can store your leftovers in there."

Jayme lifted a brow. "Can I trust you not to eat them behind my back?"

"Yes, I promise I won't. Here, I'll show you the guest room."

There were three bedrooms and two bathrooms. The master, the guest room, and the third bedroom, which was the smallest of the three that he'd converted into a home office. Only he didn't get as much work done in there as he'd hoped; the small space reminded him too much of the nursery he and Gina had decorated for Melody.

He gestured to the rooms as they went past. "My office, the master, and here's the guest room. I have a bathroom in my room, so this one is all yours."

Jayme poked her head inside. "Nice, thanks."

Ridiculous to be glad she hadn't verified the door lock. "Help yourself to anything in the kitchen, first one up makes coffee."

She smiled. "Sounds like a deal."

The hour was still relatively early, but he suspected she hadn't gotten much sleep last night either. "If you need something, let me know. I want you to be comfortable here."

"Thank you." This time her gratitude was very sincere. "I appreciate you going above and beyond for me."

"You're welcome." An unwelcome awareness shimmered between them. He took a step back, doing his best to ignore it. "Good night."

"Night."

Thankfully, she quickly disappeared into the guest room. He stood for a moment in the hallway, smiling grimly when he heard the lock click.

Logically, it made sense. A young, beautiful, single woman couldn't be too careful.

Linc told himself to be glad she was here rather than fighting off the drunk man at the Shady Lane. Yet even as he showered and crawled into bed, he couldn't help but wonder about Jayme's background. She'd mentioned how she'd met Remy Edgar and the money he'd left her and Caitlyn in his will, but he was pretty sure she'd given him a glossed-over version of the true story.

First thing in the morning, he'd dig into Marco Edgar, see if he could find any red flags indicating the guy had come back to seek revenge from Jayme. And possibly Caitlyn.

He could understand Jayme being a private person. He loved his family, but Becca drove him crazy sometimes with her matchmaking attempts. Yet it bothered him that Jayme hadn't mentioned her sister that first night.

Was Caitlyn involved? Jayme didn't think so, but it wouldn't be the first time a family member was in denial about what was happening under their nose.

Determined to find answers, he fell into an uneasy sleep.

Smoke filled the room, making his eyes burn. He couldn't stop coughing as he crawled from his bed and went to the bedroom door.

Hot! He'd recoiled from the door, remembering how they were taught in school to never open a door that was hot. That meant fire was on the other side.

His house was on fire. He scrambled toward his window and thrust it open. When he'd looked down, the ground was far, far away. But he could hear the roaring of the fire now and knew he didn't have a lot of time.

He'd have to jump.

His knees were knocking together so hard he wasn't sure he could force himself to do it. But then he heard another whooshing sound and glanced over his shoulder to see the fire was eating through his bedroom door.

Now! He threw one leg over the windowsill, then the other. He clung there with his hands, then forced himself to let go.

Falling . . . falling . . .

Linc abruptly awoke as he always did the moment he'd

jumped. Despite the chill, he was sweating as if he'd felt the heat of the blaze burning through his Spiderman pajamas.

Scrubbing his hands over his face, he took a moment to settle his heart. Why the dream had come now, tonight, was a mystery. Running toward fires and rescuing others had been his life for so many years, he'd stopped having the reoccurring nightmare. In fact, he'd often felt that becoming a firefighter had saved his life, given him a purpose after losing his parents and sister so many years ago.

Peering at the clock, he realized it was five thirty in the morning. He slid from the bed and washed up in the bathroom. After donning flannel pants and a threadbare T-shirt, he opened the door. He grinned and took a deep breath, inhaling the enticing aroma of coffee.

Apparently, Jayme was an early riser too. He padded into the kitchen in bare feet. "You're up early."

Jayme eyed him over the rim of her mug. "You too."

He nodded and pulled a mug from the cupboard, pleased at how she'd made herself at home. Maybe she was learning to trust him. "As much as I liked being a firefighter, the schedule was tough. Not sure why, but my body knows when it's daytime, making it impossible to sleep in."

"I don't think I could sleep during the day either." She set her cup down and rose. "Would you like me to make breakfast?"

Was this some strange way of paying him back for staying here? "I don't mind making breakfast. Most firefighters are good cooks, you know."

She flashed a grin. "And here I thought that was only in movies."

"Nah, we eat well when we work." It was one of the parts about the job he missed. "Sit down, I'll whip up a couple of omelets."

"Okay." She took a moment to refill her coffee cup, then sat back down. "What's the plan for today?"

"I'm going to look into Marco Edgar." He pulled eggs, cheese, veggies, and a slice of ham from the fridge. "Oh, and I'd like to meet Caitlyn."

There was a long moment of silence before Jayme responded. "I told you my sister isn't involved."

He whisked the eggs in a bowl. "Don't you think she should take precautions, just in case?"

Another long silence fell between them. He focused on making breakfast, but a sense of disappointment sliced deep.

Jayme was trying to come up with a reason for him not to talk to her sister. And the more Jayme fought against his meeting Caitlyn, the more he feared the young woman was setting the fires or knew who was.

JAYME SHOULD HAVE BEEN PREPARED for Linc's need to talk to Caitlyn. It would be a waste of time, but she realized the sooner Linc understood Caitlyn wasn't involved, the faster he'd move on to his next suspect.

Still, she was irked. "Caitlyn works weekends, so she'll be at the veterinary clinic later this morning. They don't open until nine on Saturdays."

"Good to know." He glanced at her. "She won't get in trouble if we go to the clinic, will she? We could wait until she's finished."

"The veterinarian is pretty laid-back, she won't get into trouble."

"I'm surprised they let her work as a tech if she's not finished with school."

"Much of their training is hands-on." Jayme took a sip of her coffee, trying not to sigh with pleasure. Linc stocked a high-end brand, and in her humble opinion, it was the best she'd ever tasted. "The vet, Dr. John Vice, has already hired Caitlyn and her friend Annette as full-time employees to work at the clinic when they're finished with their program."

"Hey, that's awesome news." Linc expertly folded the omelet in half. "You must be very proud."

"I am proud of her. She's grown into an amazing young woman." She paused, then added, "Which is why this visit will be a waste of time. But suit yourself."

Linc slid the two omelets onto plates and joined her at the table. "You may not realize this, but much of my work probably comes across as a waste of time. But it's important to cover every detail, if only to move on to the next suspect." He must have seen the anger flare in her eyes because he hastened to reassure her. "I don't think Caitlyn is a suspect, but she may know someone who is capable of doing this."

Jayme wanted to outright deny that possibility, but she couldn't. Caitlyn had only been in her apartment for the past five weeks, but for all Jayme knew, her younger sister could have a boyfriend by now. Or may have had a run-in with a pet owner at the clinic. She grimaced and nodded. "I see your point."

"Thank you." Linc surprised her by once again clasping his hands together and bowing his head. Flummoxed, she couldn't tear her gaze away as he murmured a prayer, just loud enough for her to hear. "Dear Lord, thank You for this food and for keeping Jayme safe in Your care. Amen."

"I . . . uh, should probably tell you that I . . . um, don't believe in God." Her declaration sounded stilted and awkward even to her own ears. "So, no need to include me in . . . that, uh, prayer." When did she talk about God and praying?

Never.

Linc's soft smile made her flush. "I'm sorry to hear you say that, Jayme. I can imagine you've traveled a long, rough road to get where you are. But you should know that I plan to include you in my prayers because I believe God is watching over you."

She had no comeback to that. Well, she did, but starting a fight didn't seem prudent. The man had allowed her to stay in his guest room, the least she could do was get along. She picked up her fork and took a bite of her omelet.

It was delicious.

Thankfully, Linc let the whole praying subject drop. They finished eating, and she helped herself to a third decadent cup of coffee before returning to her room to shower and change. When she finished, she sat on the edge of the bed and called the food pantry to let them know she wouldn't be in that morning. Irene sent a panicked note back asking if she was all right, and Jayme assured her she was and promised to make up for her absence next week.

When that chore was done, she sent a text to Caitlyn, warning her about the upcoming visit. Jayme figured her sister would be full of questions, but Caitlyn didn't reply back.

Since Caitlyn wasn't normally an early riser, she wasn't concerned. She pocketed her phone and returned to the kitchen.

Hearing water running, she assumed Linc was showering as well. She began washing their breakfast dishes, feeling foolish for the way she'd acted last night.

Of course, Linc wasn't the kind of man to ask for sex in return for a favor. The way he'd treated her at dinner had given her some insight into his character. Especially hearing about how he'd lost his wife and daughter.

So why had she overreacted? That guy in the parking lot outside the Shady Lane Motel had been what she was accustomed to dealing with. His approaching her hadn't been a surprise; in fact, she would have been suspicious if he hadn't come on to her.

She stared down at the sudsy water for a long moment. Being here in Linc's house, washing their breakfast dishes, seemed surreal. She wasn't used to sharing her living space with a man.

For thirteen years, it had been just her and Caitlyn. The two of them against the world, or so it seemed at the time. Until Remy had come into their lives, giving them the support they'd desperately needed.

Obviously, her sister's moving out had caused Jayme to experience some sort of weird regression. She'd been acting like she was still living on the streets, identifying and escaping potential predators.

Still, it was no excuse for her poor behavior. Jumping to ridiculous conclusions about Linc's motives. Of course, Linc's telling her in no uncertain terms what she was going to do hadn't helped, but to run off like that was humiliating.

She scrubbed harder and then rinsed the fry pan he'd used for the omelets. Not only had Linc given her a safe place to stay, but he'd cooked her breakfast.

Even her ex-boyfriend hadn't done anything that nice.

Then again, Eli was an ex for a reason.

As she was drying the last of the dishes, Linc returned to the kitchen. "You didn't have to do that."

"Why not? Isn't that the rule? He who cooks doesn't clean up the mess?"

He chuckled, the husky sound curling her toes. Good

grief, the man had just told her he wasn't looking for a rela-tionship, she really needed to get this crazy awareness of him under control. "Yeah, that is the firehouse rule. But we're not in the firehouse, are we?"

"Same rules should apply no matter who is cooking." She wiped her hands on the towel. "Is there something I can do to help you look into Marco Edgar?"

He hesitated, then gestured for her to follow him into the office. "Have a seat. Give me a minute to see what I can find about the guy online."

Watching someone work on the computer was bo—ring. She glanced around his office, but he didn't have any personal photos on the walls. Probably for the best as he was trying to move on.

"Is this the guy?"

She turned and peered at the screen. "Yes, that's Marco." He hadn't aged well, lines creased his features, his gray beard at odds with his dark hair, and he'd gained at least thirty pounds. "Where did you find him?"

"Social media. Looks like Marco lives the high life in California." Linc pursed his lips. "Gotta say, though, Sevierville is a long way from LA."

"I know." Jayme shrugged. "I told you it wasn't likely that he was the one behind this. As mad as he was about the ten grand, he drove a rented Corvette and had a Rolex watch on his wrist. I'm sure he's moved on by now."

"One thing I've learned from the cops in town is that those with the most money can be the worst when it comes to being cheap." Linc tapped the screen. "He's far away in LA, but that doesn't mean he didn't hire someone to lash out at you."

"How would he know enough about my past to use

fire?" Jayme asked. "And really, what's in it for him? If anything happens to me, Caitlyn gets the house."

"I'm not sure. You're not living in the same house Remy lived in, right?"

"No. The house was willed to Remy's grandkids. They sold it, and trust me, they wouldn't have sold it to me, even if I could have afforded it, which I couldn't. Not then. We've only been living in the house for the past two years."

Linc blew out a sigh. "Yeah, okay, so then I'm not sure why Marco would bother. Still, I'll keep digging see if I can find anything that might implicate him."

She nodded without holding out much hope that his effort would amount to anything. It had been her idea to mention Marco because, honestly, he had been really mad at the time of Remy's funeral. But seeing his smiling face, she couldn't imagine the guy bothering to scare her with fire over a measly ten grand.

Maybe he'd come to realize the money meant the difference between life on the street and having a future for her and Caitlyn. She'd never expected to get anything at all, which had made Remy's sweet gesture all the more heartwarming.

She worked her injured hand, massaging the fingers the way Remy had taught her. Her dexterity wasn't great, but it was better than when she'd met him.

For a moment, she remembered how painful her hand and wrist had been as she and Caitlyn escaped into the woods. She'd removed her bra and used the soft fabric to bind the burn as they'd stumbled through the woods.

If they hadn't stumbled across the caves, Jayme wasn't sure they'd have survived. Having to sleep in the cellar had been awful, but somehow, living in the caves hadn't given her the same sense of claustrophobia.

"Jayme? Are you okay?"

"Fine." She stopped massaging her hand and stood. "We should probably go soon. Maybe we can meet with Caitlyn before the clinic opens."

"Yeah, okay." Linc's gaze went back to the computer screen. "Give me a few more minutes, though. I'm almost finished checking out Marco's financial history. Seems he's in debt these days. Lots of people suing him for money."

That was interesting, although again, scaring her with fire wasn't going to bring the ten grand back. Especially since she only had about two thousand in her savings account.

She pulled out her phone, frowning when there was no response yet from Caitlyn. Her foster sister had recently turned twenty-two and was serious about her schooling and work. Caitlyn had always been finding lost or sick animals, cats, dogs, even the occasional rabbit.

"Okay, I'm ready." Linc pushed away from the computer. "Let's go."

Sitting around wasn't her style. A normal Saturday was spent working at the pantry, then cleaning the house. Sunday was laundry and cooking for the week.

Only she didn't need to cook meals for the entire week anymore now that Caitlyn was gone.

She followed Linc outside to the SUV. "When will you hear something on my car?"

"I haven't gotten over to look at it yet." He glanced at her. "It's on my list of things to do today."

"I can tell I'm holding you back. Maybe you should let me go home for the rest of the day."

"You can hang out at my place just as easily."

"No, I can't." She tried to soften her tone. "Never mind. Do you know where the veterinary clinic is located?"

"Off Greenland, right?"

"Yes." She fell silent, focusing on the vibrant yellows, reds, and oranges of the leaves changing color around them. This was normally her favorite time of the year.

Linc needed to find this arsonist, very soon. She needed to think about her future now that Caitlyn was out on her own.

As Linc pulled into the parking lot, she frowned when she didn't see Caitlyn's dark gray Honda. After checking her phone, she sighed. "Doesn't look like she's here yet."

"It's only quarter to nine." Linc shut down the car and turned to face her. "Please don't go home yet. Give me a little more time to see if I can identify this guy."

She didn't want to give in, but she reluctantly nodded. After a few minutes passed, she used her phone to call her sister. But the call went straight to voicemail.

"Cait? It's Jayme. Call me ASAP. I'm at the clinic, where are you?"

"Maybe she's running late," Linc offered.

"Maybe." But she couldn't ignore the feeling of dread. When she saw Dr. John Vice get out of his car, she pushed open the car door and ran over to him. "Dr. John? I'm sorry to bother you, but I'm looking for Caitlyn."

"Oh, she called in sick today. So did Annette." He frowned. "Thankfully, we have a light schedule or we'd really be in a bind. I have to say, it's not like your sister to do something like that."

Called in sick? He was right, that didn't sound like Caitlyn or Annette.

Jayme turned and walked slowly back to Linc's SUV, the feeling of dread growing worse with every step.

Had the arsonist turned his attention from Jayme to her younger sister?

CHAPTER FIVE

Linc noted Jayme's pale face and knew something wasn't right. "What happened?"

"We need to go to Caitlyn and Annette's apartment right now." She slammed the door. "Please, hurry."

"I need the address." She rattled it off, and he nodded, familiar with the area. He darted concerned glances at her as they left the parking lot. "I take it your sister isn't working today?"

"She and Annette called in sick." Jayme held on to the door handle with tight scarred fingers. "I'm worried about them."

"Maybe they just took off to play hooky?" Linc kept his tone reassuring, even though he was just as tense as she was.

Jayme released her grip on the door long enough to send a text. He couldn't read it from this angle, but he noticed the message was in all caps.

He prayed Caitlyn and Annette were safe. That they had indeed decided to do something fun this weekend rather than working. But knowing Jayme's work ethic, he wasn't necessarily convinced.

The small apartment building wasn't far from the veterinary clinic. He barely had the car stopped when Jayme popped out. She raked her gaze over the dozen or so parking spaces, then headed for the door.

He hurried to catch up. "Do you see her car?"

"No." Jayme pulled out her keys and used one to open the front door. Then she bolted up the stairs to the second-floor apartment. Without knocking, she unlocked the apartment door and barged in.

"Caitlyn? Annette? Are you home?"

Jayme flew through the apartment in record time, returning with a deep frown. "They're not here. And Caitlyn's car is gone, but Annette's is in the lot. I'm not sure if that's good or bad."

"That probably means they're together in Caitlyn's car." He kept his voice as reassuring as possible. "They're young, Jayme. No reason to assume the worst."

Jayme spun around and began looking more closely at the papers strewn around the kitchen table. She picked up a flyer and frowned. "Big weekend of music in Nashville."

Didn't Nashville always have live music? "Maybe a particular favorite of theirs is playing today."

Without answering, Jayme spun and disappeared into one of the bedrooms. She returned a few minutes later and sank into one of the kitchen chairs, gazing down at the flyer again. "You might be right about them going to Nashville. Caitlyn's small pink rolling suitcase is gone."

"That's good news." He crossed over and rested his hand on her shoulder. "I know it probably doesn't make you happy that she called off work, but it sounds like Caitlyn and Annette are out having fun."

"I raised her better than that," she muttered. But then

she blew out a heavy sigh and lowered her head to her hands. "I thought the arsonist grabbed her."

"I know." He hated feeling so helpless. The sooner he found this particular firebug the better. "I'm sorry you were stressed out."

After a long moment, she lifted her head and swiped at her eyes. His heart twisted at the glint of tears. "I won't relax until she responds to my text messages. Which she better do very soon."

He took Jayme's hand and gently tugged her to her feet. He drew her into his arms for a hug. "She will."

To his surprise, Jayme leaned against him. "I'm glad you decided to talk to Caitlyn, or I wouldn't have known she was gone," she said in a muffled voice.

He wanted to point out that Caitlyn was an adult but wisely kept silent. He'd only had Melody for two years, but he clearly remembered how fiercely protective he'd felt toward her.

Doubtful those feelings would have changed if his daughter had been able to grow up to become a twenty-two-year-old young woman. If anything, he figured he would have reacted worse than Jayme.

"Do you want to call the police? Ask them to keep an eye out for her car?" He lightly stroked his hand down her back.

"No." She sniffled and lifted her head to smile wryly. "I don't think the arsonist would have allowed her the time to pack a pink suitcase. I'm sure she and Annette are in Nashville having fun."

He stared into her blue eyes, then to her mouth. Even as the tiny voice in the back of his mind warned him of the danger, he lowered his head and brushed her lips with his.

Her eyes widened in surprise, but then she reached up and drew him down so they could kiss again.

Sparks flashed as heat sizzled between them. Linc wasn't sure how it was possible to react so strongly to a woman he barely knew. Especially since he didn't have room in his heart for anyone but Gina and Melody.

Jayme's phone buzzed, intruding on their kiss. She quickly stepped back, grabbing for the phone. Then she sighed in relief. "Caitlyn responded."

"Good." His voice was strained, his breathing irregular from the impact of their brief kiss. He hoped she didn't notice, glad to note Jayme was intent on texting her sister back. He took the opportunity to pull himself together.

His attempt to be supportive had backfired. This—whatever had transpired between them—couldn't happen again. It wouldn't be fair to lead Jayme on when he had no intention of going down the relationship road.

"She apologized and said they went to a music festival in Nashville. She said she'd fill me in on all the details when she gets back." Jayme smiled wanly. "I'm so relieved she and Annette are okay. Thanks for keeping me grounded through this."

"You're welcome." He edged toward the door. "Let me take you back to my place while I continue my investigation."

She hesitated, then tipped her head to the side, looking at him thoughtfully. "Actually, how about you drop me off at the food pantry instead?"

"The food pantry?" His gut tightened. "Do you need money? I can help you out . . ."

"No!" Jayme's cheeks reddened. "I volunteer there on Saturdays. I told them I couldn't come in, but I don't want to sit around your house doing nothing. That's not really my style."

"Oh, I should have known." He called himself all kinds of an idiot for jumping to that conclusion. "I—uh, can do that. If that's what you really want to do."

She locked the apartment door behind them. "I'm sure it'll be safe enough. It's not like I'll be alone."

He didn't love the idea, mostly because the firebug could easily know her regular routine. Then again, he understood her desire to be busy, to do whatever possible to keep her mind off the guy who'd already started two fires.

And likely wasn't finished yet.

He wondered what this particular arsonist wanted. Not just to start fires, but something more personal. It was as if he or she—although most arsonists were men—was actually taunting Jayme.

"Do you know where the food pantry is?" Jayme's question pulled him out of his musings.

"Yeah, the firehouse does a big food drive every Thanksgiving." He glanced at her. "I'm surprised we didn't meet before now."

She shrugged. "You probably didn't notice me."

He couldn't imagine that was possible. Granted, he'd been happily married to Gina at the time, but Jayme was incredibly beautiful and surely would have been noticed by the firefighters who were single.

She opened and closed her right hand. "My scars tend to hold some men back. I've gotten used to it, but when seen for the first time . . ." She shrugged. "I've noticed it's off-putting."

"That's ridiculous." He had trouble believing any guy could be that shallow. "The scars are barely noticeable."

She lifted a brow. "You're being nice, but it's not necessary. I've lived with them for a long time. I'm used to the repulsed looks."

"Idiots," he muttered. The drive to the food pantry took another ten minutes, and when he pulled up in front of the place, he was reluctant to let her go. "Will you call me if you need something?"

"Uh, sure." She appeared flustered at the suggestion, no doubt because of their brief yet potent kiss. "Give me your cell number."

He recited the information while she plugged it into her phone. Then she called him so that he could add her name and number to his contact list. "Don't worry about me, I'll be fine."

Jayme hopped out of his vehicle and headed inside. He thought it was honorable of her to spend her Saturday's volunteering at the food pantry. There was so much about her that he still didn't know.

When she disappeared from view, he put the vehicle into gear and headed to the police garage where her Ford Fiesta was waiting.

He needed to stay focused on figuring out who was behind these fires and why Jayme had been targeted.

Because he already liked Jayme Weston far too much for his peace of mind.

SHE NEVER SHOULD HAVE KISSED him.

Jayme enjoyed helping out at the food pantry, but it wasn't as if the work was difficult. When she'd arrived, Irene had been surprised but had gratefully left her to take over. Irene was the woman in charge, but Jayme didn't mind when she'd announced she was leaving. Jayme preferred working alone.

Yet stocking shelves and helping those who came in for food wasn't enough to keep her mind from ruminating over what had transpired in Caitlyn's apartment.

She'd kissed Linc. Okay, he'd kissed her first, but that brief taste hadn't been enough. Oh, no, she'd pulled him down and thrown herself at him. As if she'd never been kissed before in her life.

The poor man had made it clear he wasn't interested. Had lost his wife and daughter, so she didn't blame him. She'd always been a loner, had never allowed herself to get close to anyone, except of course to Caitlyn. So why had she acted so out of character?

No clue.

Whatever. She needed to find a way to ignore this weird attraction she felt toward him because she had no doubt the man would break her heart.

If she let him.

"Anything else?" Jayme smiled at the young woman carrying a toddler on her hip and holding another child by the hand.

"No, this is fine, thanks." The woman turned to leave, and Jayme couldn't help but wish there was more she could do to help the struggling single mother. The same way Remy Edgar had helped her.

Why not put Caitlyn's old room to good use? The moment the idea popped into her mind, she felt a surge of excitement.

Yes, that was the answer. She could pay Remy's generosity forward by helping someone less fortunate. It was about time she let her younger sister move on with her life. The fact that Caitlyn and Annette had blown off work to attend some fall music festival in Nashville was proof her sister was doing just that. After pushing aside the fear, worry, and yeah, annoyance, Jayme was glad her sister was out having fun.

Fun had been in short supply over the past thirteen years. At least for Jayme. She'd sheltered Caitlyn from most of the bad stuff whenever possible. Not all of it, after all, Caitlyn had lived with the Preacher too. But Caitlyn had been nine when they'd escaped, compared to Jayme's sixteen.

From what Jayme could tell, Caitlyn had been able to repress most of the memories from those awful years. Caitlyn hadn't been there as long, only two years, which may have helped. Jayme had been there six years, most of the other fosters had come within the next year after her first. At first she'd been thrilled to have other kids living there, thinking their presence would make things better. Only it hadn't. Instead, the environment had gone from bad to worse. The more kids, the more the Preacher ranted and raved. She'd never understood why he'd brought more kids into his home in the first place. Money, probably, although she felt there was something sick and twisted going on in his mind.

The Preacher had chosen his abuse targets wisely, lashing out at Caitlyn only when the older kids tried to rebel.

His strategy had worked. They'd all grown very protective of Caitlyn. And learned very quickly to toe the line.

Until the night of the fire.

"Miss? Is it okay if I take these?"

Jayme realized another young woman had come into the pantry. Someone she didn't recognize. "Good morning, my name is Jayme. Of course, help yourself to whatever you need."

"I'm Renee. There's a lot of stuff here." The way the woman glanced around indicated it was her first trip to the pantry.

Jayme came out from behind the counter, smiling gently. "I know, but I promise you can help yourself. There's no limit as to what you can take. We understand you may have a family at home."

"I—didn't expect to see so much variety." Renee looked younger than Caitlyn, except for her eyes, which had seen far too much. Jayme understood, she'd had the same experiences. She subtly checked for signs of drug use but didn't see anything obvious like dilated pupils, needle marks, or meth-stained teeth.

"Are you new to the area, Renee?" Jayme kept her question casual, lest she scare her off. Runaways were skittish, trying to avoid unwanted attention.

Renee nodded but moved toward the tall shelf containing canned goods and boxed milk. All food donations were nonperishable, and Jayme often wished she could provide something more nutritious.

When the young woman's arms were full of canned goods, a jar of peanut butter, and a box of dried milk, Jayme picked up a box and began packing her items. "You still have some room if you need more."

"I'm fine, but I have to ask, who brings all this food in?"

"Donations are from citizens who live in the area." Jayme smiled. "We're open every Saturday, so you're welcome to come back next weekend."

"I—thanks." Renee picked up her box and hurried out.

Jayme thought someone like Renee might be the perfect candidate to stay in Caitlyn's old room, but she couldn't even think about that until the stupid arsonist was caught. No sense in putting others in danger because some crazy guy liked setting fires.

The pantry closed at 1:00 p.m., and most of the people who came on a regular basis knew that. By twelve thirty, the place was empty. Jayme went back to straightening the shelves, putting the items that remained in order.

When the door opened ten minutes later, she glanced over in surprise as she recognized one of the physical therapy clinic patients step across the threshold. He was roughly in his early sixties and had a deep jagged scar on his face and others along his left arm. She didn't know the details about his care and treatment as he worked primarily with Sandra during his weekly appointment. "Hi, Mr. Shepard. Can I help you with something?"

"Oh, I just wanted to check the place out. And here." He crossed over and set two cans of green beans on the counter. "I thought you might be able to use these."

"Thanks, we are always happy to accept donations." She thought it was sweet of him to bring in something when his worn clothes indicated he didn't have money to spare. She took the cans and set them next to the other canned vegetables. "Take a look around, there's plenty left if you need something in particular."

"Thank you, Ms. Jayme." He peered at her through thick glasses and smiled, the deeply grooved scar running down his left cheek meant that only one side of his mouth tipped up. Knowing how people couldn't look at her scarred hand made her feel bad for the guy who had even more disfiguring scars.

The first time she'd seen him, she'd wondered what had happened to him. Sandra had confided that he'd had several surgeries after a close encounter with a bomb. Even that much was probably breaking privacy laws, so Jayme hadn't pushed for more. She thought he might be a soldier, but he looked almost too frail for that. The man shuffled over to the shelving units, moving as if he'd broken his hip at some point.

"I'll take some peanut butter, if that's okay." He turned and held the jar in his hand. "I love peanut butter."

"Who doesn't?" she asked with a smile. "Of course, help yourself. Have a good day."

"You too, Ms. Jayme." He shuffled toward the door. "You too."

After Mr. Shepard left, she used her phone to call Linc. It felt weird to call him, but she was determined to treat him as a friend, despite the devastating kiss.

"Hi, Jayme, everything okay?"

"Fine. I'm getting ready to close for the day."

"Okay, I'll be there soon."

"Did you find anything?" She hated to keep asking, but she didn't want to stay at Linc's house one moment longer than necessary. She was already dreading the fact that she'd need to spend the rest of the day there.

All that togetherness would wreak havoc on her ability to keep him firmly in the friendship corner of her mind.

"I'll fill you in later. Give me about fifteen minutes to get there."

"Okay, thanks." She disconnected from the call and debated whether or not to head back home. Spending the night in Linc's guest room had seemed prudent so soon after the car fire.

But now she wondered if doing so was really necessary.

She closed up the pantry at one o'clock sharp, then sent a text to Irene to let her know things had gone well. Irene responded with a smiley face and a heart.

A minute later, Linc's black SUV pulled into the parking lot. Her heart did a little flip at the sight of him.

Stop it, she chided. *He's not yours, remember?*

He pulled up beside her. She opened the door and climbed in. "Hungry? The Red Mill has a special on ribs today."

"Ah, sure." She sternly reminded herself his casual invite to share a meal wasn't a date. "While we eat, you can fill me in on what you've learned after investigating the fire that damaged my car."

"It's not much," he warned. "But I found one interesting link between the two fires."

Only one? She tried not to let her disappointment show. "I guess that's better than nothing."

He glanced at her. "It's a slow process, one that unfortunately can't be rushed."

"I know. I guess I'm just impatient to get my life back." She rubbed her scarred hand. "You know, I'm glad Caitlyn is in Nashville over the weekend. Maybe you'll catch this guy before she returns."

"Gee, no pressure," Linc said dryly.

That made her chuckle. "Sorry, I don't mean to be a pest, but you know." She waved a hand. "I'm sure you'd like to get this guy behind bars as much as I do."

"True." He sent her a sidelong glance. "It's important that you're safe, Jayme. I'm worried this guy will strike again."

"That's the only reason I agreed to stay in your guest room last night." She shifted in her seat. "I was hoping you'd found enough that I could return home."

"Not yet. I know it's not easy being in a stranger's house, but humor me for a while longer, okay?"

She nodded because really, it's not as if she had much of a choice.

Linc parked in the crowded parking lot. The barbequed spare rib special must be a large draw because they had to wait fifteen minutes before they were seated.

After they placed their order, Linc leaned over the table and dropped his voice. "I can tell you that both the smoke bomb and the car fire were definitely done by the same person."

"Smoke bomb?" She frowned. "You mean the first one wasn't a fire?"

"No, it was. The small fire was contained, though. What I found interesting was that the chemicals used were specifically combined in a way to create more smoke than actual fire."

"Great, I called the fire department for nothing."

"You absolutely did the right thing," he corrected. "You had no way of knowing the source of the smoke. Don't ever hesitate to call the fire department." He flashed a smile. "You know we firefighters thrive on adrenaline. Even a false alarm is better than sitting around and staring at each other."

His attempt to make her feel better was sweet. "Okay, so why do you think the smoke bomb and the car fire were similar?"

"Same types of chemicals, only they were constructed in different ways. The car fire was set with an accelerant, which was different, yet other parts of the fire were similar. Including the fact that it was relatively contained." He stared at her for a long moment. "I'll be honest, it's not typical for a firebug to deliberately create a small fire. For them, bigger is always better."

"You're the expert," she agreed. "So basically, this guy is just trying to scare me."

He shrugged. "I'm not convinced. I hate to say this, but it's more like he's toying with you. Taunting you. Trying to knock you off balance, to keep you afraid."

"Thanks, but I already knew that. I just wish I knew who was responsible." She toyed with her napkin, then grimaced. "I want it to be Marco Edgar, but you're probably going to rule him out soon enough."

"He's been in LA all week," Linc admitted. "No way he could have flown from LA to Knoxville and back."

"I figured." Marco had been mad at her, upset about some *nobody like her* getting money from his dad, but starting fires didn't seem his style.

"He could have hired someone, so he's not completely off the hook," Linc said. "Although his being in debt could work against that theory too. If starting these fires doesn't provide some sort of financial payoff, not sure he'd bother."

Good thing this wasn't a date because everything he'd told her so far had been one big Debbie Downer. "So basically, you're no closer to finding out who did this."

He winced. "I've put the information I've gathered from the investigation into a country-wide arson database. If there are similar fires out there, we might get a lead on our firebug."

Or maybe his arson database would spit out nothing at all.

Their server came with their meals, tangy chicken for her and of course spicy barbecued ribs for Linc. She picked up her fork, then set it down when she saw him bow his head to pray.

Seriously, who did this kind of thing before every single

meal? She felt certain he was only doing it because she wasn't a believer.

"Lord, please bless this food and continue keeping us safe in Your care. We ask for Your guidance as we seek to find those responsible for these fires. Amen."

She almost asked him to include Caitlyn next time, before remembering the idea of praying wasn't her deal. Although if she ever would succumb to praying, it would be something she'd do for Caitlyn.

Not for herself.

Silence fell as they dug into their meals. Jayme sipped her water, trying not to notice how enthusiastically Linc enjoyed his ribs.

"You wanna try them?" He grinned. "These ribs are the best in the city."

"I'll take your word for it." She speared a piece of her chicken with a fork. "Mine is really good too."

Above the din of the packed restaurant, she heard the faint whine of a siren. Curious, she craned her neck to look out the window.

"It's a fire truck," Linc said with a frown.

"How do you know?"

"Different sound than a police siren." He reached for his phone. "No call yet, so it's probably nothing."

"Maybe a cat is stuck in a tree." Her weak attempt at a joke fell flat.

His phone rang, and her stomach tightened as he quickly answered. "Where?" Another pause, then he said, "I'm on my way."

"It's a real fire?" she asked, even though the grim expression on his face told the story.

"Yes. We have to go." He pulled out a wad of cash and left it on the table.

"Go where?" She grabbed her purse and hurried to keep up.

"The physical therapy clinic." He glanced at her as they jogged toward his car.

The clinic? "They're not open on Saturdays."

Linc didn't reply but drove as quickly as possible to the physical therapy clinic where she worked. Despite preparing herself mentally, she still gasped in horror.

The front window was broken, revealing the interior of the clinic full of flames.

CHAPTER SIX

Linc felt sick as he pulled over behind the fire truck and watched the flames feed off the interior of the physical therapy clinic. He had no idea how large the inside of the place was. Based on what he could see through the large front window, he feared the clinic might be a total loss.

Why had the arsonist chosen the physical therapy clinic as his next target?

Just because Jayme worked there? Or was it possible one of the patients was setting fires as a way to get back at the employees?

"I . . . can't believe it." Jayme's voice was barely a whisper.

"I'm sorry." Linc knew the words were inadequate. He was relieved to know the place was closed, so there were no potential casualties. Yet he still felt as if he'd let her down. He'd asked the police to keep an eye on her house but hadn't considered the clinic as a possible target. Not that it would have mattered if he had. The small police department wasn't staffed for twenty-four-hour surveillance. "Stay here, I need to talk to the captain."

"I'm coming with you." She pushed out of the SUV before he could stop her. And really, he couldn't blame her. If this fire was a result of someone trying to get back at her, he'd want to know exactly what was going on too.

"Captain." Linc nodded at Barstow, the police captain on duty. "What do you know so far?"

"Looks to be a type of Molotov cocktail tossed through the window, causing the interior to go up in flames." Captain Barstow glanced at Jayme. "Once we verified no one was inside, our goal has been to keep the fire under control and prevent it from spreading to other businesses nearby."

Jayme's face was pale as she turned to look at the clothing shop, Brenda's Boutique, located within ten feet of the clinic. Customers from the boutique and other nearby businesses milled around, obviously having been evacuated for their safety. Linc noted one fire crew kept a stream of water deployed on the boutique as the closest place to the source of the fire. The rest of the firefighters on scene continued battling the blaze.

"Any idea what accelerant was used?" Linc asked.

"We believe kerosene was the source, at least from the smell." Captain Barstow shrugged. "We have police officers canvassing the area, checking IDs and searching for anyone reeking of accelerant or showing too much interest in the fire."

Linc nodded, taking a moment to do his own visual sweep of the area. Nobody stood out as not belonging, but he knew from experience the firebug was likely out there watching.

From a distance, using binoculars? Maybe. He took his time, searching likely vantage points but didn't see anything remotely suspicious.

This particular firebug wasn't following any normal pattern, so for all he knew, the guy was long gone. Sitting somewhere private and safe while he planned his next target.

One that might hit closer to home.

Another wave of nausea hit hard at the thought. "I should have anticipated this," he said in a low voice. "The two small fires had been engineered to get our attention, but this?" He shook his head helplessly. "This is full-out, in-your-face arson."

"It's hard to imagine anyone setting fire to the clinic as a way to get back at me," Jayme murmured. "Why lash out at a place that helps patients who have been hurt? Seeing this" —she waved at the fire—"makes me realize Marco Edgar probably isn't involved. It just doesn't make any sense."

The fact that Marco hadn't left the state of California meant he wasn't the one who'd set the fire. But even if he had hired someone, the clinic was a strange target. "I know, but I'm not ruling anyone out at this point." Not that proving who was or wasn't involved would be easy. There were cases where people went out to hire an arsonist, mostly for insurance reasons. Was it possible that Marco knew enough about Jayme that he thought striking out at her place of employment would hurt her financially? Revenge could be as much of a motivator as money.

More so in the case of a very personal vendetta.

A good ten minutes passed before the fire crew had the blaze under control. Unfortunately, the scene would be too hot for him to begin investigating.

"I guess I won't be getting paid anytime soon." Jayme's blue eyes were dazed as she stared at the damaged clinic. "The other employees either. It's all so surreal. I'm not the only one who will suffer. Everyone who works here will be negatively impacted from this."

"Try not to worry about that now." He put his arm around her shoulders, giving her a gentle hug. "The clinic has insurance. I'm sure the goal will be to get things up and running as soon as possible. It will just take some time."

"Okay." She abruptly shrugged off his arm and walked back toward the SUV. He wanted to follow but sensed she needed some time alone.

"Jayme? Can you believe this?" He turned at the sound of a woman's voice. A pretty African American woman rushed toward Jayme and hugged her. "I don't know what to think. Could Gary have done this?"

Gary? Linc moved closer.

"I don't know, Sandra. I—I think it's my fault." Jayme's voice broke as tears streamed down her face. "I think someone has targeted me."

"What? Why would you say that?" Sandra cradled Jayme, then eyed Linc curiously as he joined them. "Do you know why Jayme thinks this is her fault?"

"My name is Lincoln Quade, and I'm the fire investigator." He offered what he hoped was a reassuring smile. "There have been two other incidents, one at Jayme's home and another involving setting her car on fire. We have reason to believe this recent incident is related to the others."

"Whaaat?" Sandra pulled back and gaped at Jayme. "Why didn't you say something?"

Jayme swiped at her tears. "There's nothing you can do."

"But you could have told me." Sandra put her hands on her hips. "Or came to stay with us for a while."

"And put you and George in danger?" Jayme sniffled and shook her head. "Not a chance."

"She's staying with me," Linc said. "I'll keep her safe."

Sandra eyed him curiously. "I'll hold you to that." Then she looked back at the smoldering clinic. Her shoulders slumped. "Not sure what's going to happen now."

"It's all my fault," Jayme said.

"No, it's the arsonist's fault," Linc corrected. "You're the innocent victim in this."

"The entire staff at the clinic are the true innocent victims." Jayme pulled away and raked her hand through her hair. "I feel awful."

"Linc?" He turned when the captain called out his name. He left the women and crossed over to join him.

"What's up?"

"We're going to clear the scene soon," Captain Barstow told him. "You won't be able to get in to investigate, though, until tomorrow."

"I know. Did you hear about the other incidents?"

Barstow nodded. "The smoke bomb and the car fire." He glanced at the blackened clinic. "This is a big step up from that."

"No kidding. It's a much bigger message, although interesting that he chose to throw the firebomb when the place was closed." A conscientious firebug? Nah, he didn't believe it. No, this was just another attempt to scare Jayme.

"Small blessings," Barstow said.

"Yes, but the worst part of all is that he's not finished. Not by a long shot."

Barstow's gaze narrowed. "You think her house is next?"

"Don't you?"

Barstow whistled under his breath. "Well, if that's true,

you need to find him. Before he moves from torching empty buildings to those with people inside." He jerked his thumb over his shoulder. "Like your friend Jayme over there."

"That's the plan." As he looked at what was left of the physical therapy clinic, he made a silent promise to protect Jayme, with his own life if necessary.

She didn't deserve any of this. No matter what she thought, none of these fires were her fault.

"Linc?" Jayme came over to stand beside him. "I'd like to go home."

"Please don't." He took her arm and drew her toward his SUV. "I understand your concern, but I don't want you to be anywhere near that house if he decides to target that next."

"But the entire house will burn to the ground if no one is there to report the fire the minute it starts." Her gaze implored him to understand. "Better that I'm there to sound the alarm than to lose everything."

"Your life is all that matters." He opened the passenger door for her. "We'll talk about this later, but keep in mind all the items in your house can be replaced. You can't."

She sighed and climbed into the car. He shut the door behind her and resisted the urge to scream in frustration.

No way was he going to allow Jayme to stay at her house, lying in wait for the arsonist to show up.

If she had somewhere else to stay, though. Like maybe with Sandra and George, he could do that for her.

Anything to keep her safe.

JAYME COULDN'T GET the smell of smoke out of her nose, her clothes, or her head. Watching the flames had reminded her of the Preacher's cabin all those years ago.

The fire had been terrifying, even though it had also provided the freedom she and the other fosters had so desperately needed. If the Preacher hadn't tried to rape her, the fire wouldn't have happened.

Yet looking back, she couldn't help but be relieved things had turned out the way they did. The burn scars on her right hand and wrist were well worth the price of freedom.

Not just her freedom, but all of the fosters who'd escaped that night.

She couldn't summon the energy to argue when Linc drove to his place. As much as she wanted to protect her house, she knew he was right.

A home, clothes, and other personal items could be replaced.

It wasn't like she had anything with strong sentimental value. Living on the streets, the sleazy motel, and then the dilapidated trailer did not encourage dragging a lot of personal stuff along with you.

Especially because of the roaches.

Jayme followed Linc into the house. The urge to return to her own space was strong, but she told herself to get over it. One thing she'd learned over the years was never get too attached to things. Although she'd worked so hard for that house, to provide a home for Caitlyn.

"Jayme, will you please sit down for a few minutes?"

One glance at Linc's serious expression had her sinking into the closest kitchen chair. "I know what you're going to say."

"You do?" He arched an eyebrow.

She curled her scarred hand into a fist. "You think the fire thirteen years ago is part of this. And I would probably agree with you, if not for the fact that the Preacher and his wife died that night."

"The Preacher?" Linc stared in shock. "Maybe you should start at the beginning."

Swallowing hard, she nodded. He deserved that much, although she'd rarely spoken of that night. After she and Caitlyn had escaped, they'd pretty much left the past behind. Nothing to be gained by ruminating over it. "I lived with a total of six other foster kids, including Caitlyn, with a horrible man who called himself the Preacher. He physically and verbally abused us, ranting and raving about how we were all terrible sinners who were going to hell."

"That's not like any preacher I've ever heard," Linc said gently. "God isn't vengeful. He is loving and patient and kind."

"Yeah, well, that's not what the Preacher pounded into us on a daily basis." When it looked like Linc was going to argue, she waved a hand. "Whatever, that part doesn't really matter." She forced herself to meet his gaze. "One night, the Preacher decided he was going to rape me. I could tell it was coming, he used to touch me . . ." She looked away, unable to put the revulsion she'd felt at his touch into words. The weird little circle thing he did with his index finger around her elbow had made her want to throw up. "I'm not sure what set him off that night. He was acting weird, worse than usual. He grabbed at me, pinning me against the sofa, whispering about how it was time for me to make him happy. When he began unfastening his pants, I reached over, grabbed the oil lamp, and swung it at his head, hitting him with all the strength I possessed."

"Dear God, Jayme." Linc reached over to take her hands in his. "That's how you were burned?"

"Yes. The Preacher screamed in pain, trying to get away from the burning oil, while I took the opportunity to get the other fosters out of the cellar."

"He . . . forced you to sleep in the cellar?"

She pushed on. "The cabin filled with thick smoke very fast; it seemed to go up in flames faster than I thought possible. We barely had time to escape. But all of us managed to get outside. We watched the cabin burn." She paused, then added, "The Preacher and his wife didn't make it out."

Linc tightened his hands around hers. "I can't even begin to tell you how sorry I am that you had to endure such an awful event. No one should have to go through such a thing, especially not a child."

"Thanks. But Caitlyn and I survived and thrived." She tried to smile. "With the help of wonderful people like Remy Edgar."

"I know you won't want to hear this, but God was watching out for you, Jayme. Watching out for all of you."

She wasn't ready to admit that, although getting away had seemed like a herculean task. "I was the oldest of the fosters. Sawyer and Hailey were the second oldest, then Darby, then Cooper and Trent. Caitlyn was the youngest. When we decided to split up to avoid getting caught and thrown back into the foster system, I kept Caitlyn with me."

"You're amazing, Jayme. I can't imagine it was easy for the two of you to overcome that horror."

"Well, after you've been in hell, you learn to appreciate having a roof over your head." She smiled. "Even that of a roach-infested motel."

"I had no idea. What you went through makes my life seem like a cakewalk."

"Losing your wife and daughter was far worse. It's not like any of us grieved over losing the Preacher or Ruth."

"Jayme, I appreciate you trusting me with this story." Linc's dark eyes clung to hers. "But I have to ask, how do you know for sure the Preacher and his wife didn't survive the fire?"

She couldn't blame him for doubting that part of her story. The minute she'd learned of the contained fire outside her house, she'd fleetingly considered the Preacher. "The cabin was deep in the woods outside Cherokee, North Carolina. Far enough from others that no one would know what went on there every day. We all huddled outside the cabin, watching as it burned. None of us tried to go inside to save them."

"No one would blame you for that," he hastened to reassure her.

"The point is, the Preacher stumbled toward his bedroom, I assume to get a blanket to douse the fire. His wife was already asleep, she didn't seem to hear the commotion as we got out of the cabin, so maybe she was drugged. It wouldn't surprise me, I wouldn't put anything past the Preacher."

"But there was more than one way out of the cabin, right?" Linc pressed. "How do you know they didn't escape out the back?"

"Because we went out the back door. The cellar was in the kitchen." She drew in a long breath, forcing herself to tell him the rest. Every last, awful, detail. "As I told you, the fire started in the living room. In a very short time, it spread from the sofa onto the chair, reaching all the way to the wood-paneled walls." She could see how the flames had raced upward, like tiny fiery fairies. "There was a fire in the stone fireplace too, although that was emitting more smoke than usual."

"Why was that?"

"I'm not sure, I think the logs might have been wet." She remembered how the smoke had burned her eyes, making them water. And how strange it had been that the Preacher hadn't noticed. Maybe he was too intent on what he'd wanted to do to her. She shied away from that thought. "The front door was in the living room. The last time I saw the Preacher, he was headed into his bedroom and"—she swallowed hard—"he was still on fire."

Linc surprised her by lifting her scarred hand to his mouth, pressing a soft kiss to her rigid, bumpy skin.

She told herself not to read too much into his sweet gesture. Linc was a very nice guy, he'd care about anyone telling this story. "The entire time we were outside, we watched for any sign of the Preacher or his wife. We expected them to come out, but they never did. Frankly, I don't see how they could have escaped."

"But you don't know that they didn't," he insisted. "What if they went out a window?"

"We would have seen them. Even though it was night-time, the fire lit up the entire area so that we would have seen them staggering away from the house."

"How long did you watch?"

Forever. Or so it seemed. She thought back, then slowly shook her head. "I can't say for sure, but we didn't take off until we heard the fire truck sirens. At that point, we huddled together, discussing our options. We all agreed to never go back into the system, but we also knew that seven kids hanging together would be too noticeable. So we decided to split up and disappear into the woods. Sawyer, Cooper, and Trent went south. Hailey and Darby went west. Caitlyn and I headed northwest." She met his gaze. "Living out in the wilderness made it easy for us to disappear, never to be heard from again."

He nodded slowly. "I can understand that goal. And that's why you didn't get proper treatment for your burned hand."

"Yes." She shrugged. "Remy was a retired physical therapist. He noticed the scars and gave me exercises to do. He also sneaked me into the clinic for other treatments. I owe him a lot. My hand is much better now than it was when we first met."

"There aren't enough words to describe how much I admire you." Linc's low, husky voice sent tingles of awareness down her spine. "You're the strongest woman I've ever known. And what you've done for your sister Caitlyn is equally amazing."

"Anyone else would have done the same thing." She wasn't used to this kind of attention. Then again, she'd never told anyone the details of her past.

"Does the Preacher have a real name?"

Linc's question caught her off guard. "I—yes. I believe his name was Simon. At least, that's how Ruth referred to him at one point. Simon and Ruth Penske."

"Give me a few minutes to do a quick search on them." He released her hands to get up from the table. He grabbed his computer and returned, opening it and jiggling the mouse to bring it to life.

"You're not going to find them." She knew in her bones they'd died that night. If they hadn't, she firmly believed the Preacher would have found her long before now. Or maybe he'd been burned so badly he couldn't do much of anything. Which would include coming to Sevierville and starting fires to scare her.

Still, curiosity won out, and she went over to sit beside Linc while he worked. Seeing their names in the search bar brought an idea. "Maybe you should search for their obituary. Someone may have held a funeral for them. They certainly had the people at the department of health and human services fooled, otherwise they'd never have been given seven foster kids to care for."

"The Preacher didn't have his own church or congregation?" Linc asked.

"He did, but it was very small. One year we received Christmas gifts from the parishioners." She shrugged. "The Preacher made us attend Sunday service, it was the only time we were seen in public, dressed nicely as we were told to. But we were warned that if we disobeyed or tried to get someone's attention, we'd be sorry. Having lived through his beatings, kneeling for hours as he ranted and raved was bad enough. None of us were anxious to experience the full extent of his wrath. Besides, once Caitlyn came to live with us, he threatened to hurt her as a way to make the rest of us behave." She grimaced. "That worked better than anything because she was only seven years old at the time."

Linc paused to look at her. "Seven years old and he threatened to hurt her. What kind of monster was he?"

"The worst kind." Reliving the memories wasn't fun. "Now you can see why I don't pray. The Preacher went on and on about how God would punish us, and truthfully, his words struck home. After all, we must have been sent to live with him for a reason, right? We were there as punishment for everything we did wrong."

"No, that's not true." Linc turned in his seat to face her. "He lied to you, Jayme. Children are innocent; God was not punishing you. Not then, and not now. That madman was a liar, and I'm glad you hit him with that lantern. Although I wish you wouldn't have suffered a burn in the process."

His declaration was sweet. "Maybe." She couldn't deny that it was easier to believe that now than back then. But she still didn't quite believe God existed. And if He did, then why had He waited so long to help set them free?

"I know the Preacher was lying to you, and I wish you could come to know God the way I do. It hurts me to know how much you and the other kids suffered at that man's hands." Linc turned his attention back to the computer. "Okay, let's see what I can dig up on these two. Just so that I can cross them off the suspect list. This happened thirteen years ago, in Cherokee, North Carolina, right?"

"Yes." She didn't harbor any illusions about what Linc would find. She watched him work for a few minutes but couldn't concentrate. Feeling restless, she stood and moved over to look out the window. For the first time, she noticed Linc's house had a nice view of the forest.

The trees, the caverns she and Caitlyn had found back when they'd first escaped had been her sanctuary. But living in the cold without shelter from the elements soon wore on them. Especially Caitlyn. The caverns had worked for a few weeks, but finally, they'd been forced to move.

To find civilization.

Yet they hadn't wanted to go far. Something about the Smoky Mountains called to her. If she had her way, she'd never leave.

But Caitlyn? That her sister had gone to Nashville with Annette made Jayme wonder if Caitlyn was getting restless being confined to such a small town. Maybe her sister longed to live somewhere else. Someplace bigger, with more action. Lots of young people.

Easy to understand if she did, but not as easy to let her sister go.

She leaned her forehead against the glass, thinking about Caitlyn's future. Maybe she should sell the house, use the proceeds to help pay for more college. Caitlyn insisted she would be happy as a veterinary tech, but Jayme felt certain her little sister would really prefer to be a full-fledged veterinarian.

Yet even getting the bachelor's degree would be tough, and getting into the program was highly competitive. While Jayme had done everything possible to keep Caitlyn enrolled in school during the past thirteen years, the two years of being homeschooled by Ruth had caused Caitlyn to fall behind. It was all her sister could do to keep up even with the teacher spending extra time with her.

But was it fair to put a price on her sister's dreams?

No, it wasn't.

"Jayme? Take a look at this."

She turned and hurried over to see what he'd found. Linc turned the computer so she could see the screen head-on.

Searching for the obituary had worked. There in black and white was proof that Simon and Ruth Penske were dead.

The date was October 3, the same day as the fire.

She sat back in the chair. "I told you they were dead."

"Yeah, but you didn't read it all the way through." Linc tapped on the screen. "They're presumed to have died in the fire. The fire burned so hot for so long, there wasn't much left behind. Only a few human remains were found, but not enough to identify them."

A chill rippled over her. "So you're saying they may not be dead?"

"I'm saying, anything is possible."

She shook her head, unwilling to believe it. Because even if the Preacher had survived, he'd have needed medical care. The guy wouldn't be able to be in a hospital for massive burns without anyone knowing who he was.

Could he?

CHAPTER SEVEN

Linc stared at Simon and Ruth Penske's obituary, his thoughts whirling. Logically, he knew the chance of the Preacher or his wife surviving the fire Jayme had described was slim to none. Especially if she'd thrown the lantern at the Preacher. His clothes must have caught on fire, and the burns he'd sustained must have been severe. No doubt, he'd have been the one who'd died, before Ruth.

Yet he couldn't dismiss the possibility.

"Let's say you're right and the Preacher somehow managed to survive." Jayme folded her arms across her chest. "Why would he wait thirteen years to come find me? And really, why not just torch my house while I was sleeping and be done with it? The Preacher was never subtle. Quite the opposite."

He hated knowing the man who professed to be a Preacher of the Bible and of God's word had instead abused the children in his care and attempted to rape Jayme. Burning to death in his own home was probably too good for him. Listening to her story without pulling her into his arms and holding her had been the most difficult thing he'd ever done.

And her inner strength, the way she'd gone through the next thirteen years to be sitting here now working as a physical therapy tech and supporting her sister's education only made him admire her more. He tried to focus on what she'd said rather than his desire to kiss her.

"This is all theory and conjecture. It's likely the Preacher and his wife are truly dead. But if he wasn't, he'd need a lot of time to recover from his numerous injuries, then he'd have to find you. Which wouldn't be easy since you'd left North Carolina, escaping through the Smoky Mountains into Tennessee." He shrugged. "As to why he's dragging this out over time? The man is certifiably crazy. I don't think logic will ever explain what he's thinking, what he's feeling."

The only thing Linc knew for certain was that if the Preacher had survived, he definitely had a reason to seek revenge against Jayme.

She rose to her feet and moved back toward the window, staring out at the beautiful trees turning red, yellow, and orange. After a long moment, she turned to face him. "If the Preacher is alive and here in Sevierville, then I'll know him when I see him. He won't be able to sneak up on me."

"Understood. But this is why I'd rather have you stay here with me." He held her gaze. "Don't go back to your place. Not yet."

She frowned. "Why do I think you'll still be saying that tomorrow, Monday, and even a week from now?"

He couldn't deny it. "Tomorrow, I'll head back to the physical therapy clinic to begin my investigation. It's very likely the person who threw the Molotov cocktail is the same one responsible for the smoke bomb and car fire. The police are canvassing the area; they may come up with a witness since the firebomb was tossed into the clinic in broad daylight."

She sighed and shook her head. "I don't know. It still seems more likely that I'll catch him in the act if I'm staying at my place."

"Give law enforcement some time to do their job." He hoped she didn't notice the undertone of panic in his tone. If she insisted on returning home, he planned on going with her. If she didn't let him in the house, he'd sleep in his car.

Jayme grimaced and nodded slowly. "Okay, I'll stay one more night."

His shoulders slumped with relief. "Good. Now that we're in agreement on that, I'd like to keep searching for arsonists who are known to work for hire before we figure out what to do for dinner."

"Sure." Her attempt at a smile was weak.

"Do you want to watch a movie? Or read a book? I have several mystery novels if you're interested."

"Mysteries?" She brightened at that idea. "I'd love to see what you have."

He grinned, ridiculously pleased to have stumbled upon a shared interest. "Come with me. I have a bunch of them in my room."

She knelt in front of his bookcase, touching the book spines as she reviewed them. "I've read these, they're great, aren't they? Oh wait, here's an author I've never read." She pulled the book out from the others. He was pleased she'd chosen a Christian suspense.

"You'll love it," he assured her. "But if you don't, there are others to choose from."

"I normally get books from the library." She rose to her feet. "Thanks for letting me borrow this one."

"You're more than welcome. In fact, you can borrow my books anytime." He made the offer as if they'd be seeing each other once the danger from this particular firebug was over.

She eyed him curiously but returned to the living room. As he sat at his computer, she curled up in the corner of his sofa. He liked having her there and knew spending time with her like this was something he could get used to.

Focus, he told himself sternly. They were friends. Being thrown together had brought a camaraderie he hoped might continue.

But he wouldn't, couldn't allow it to go any further than that.

As he worked, Linc found two distinct possible suspects. Terrance Foley, a known arsonist who'd gotten out of prison earlier this year. Foley's address was listed as Memphis, which was on the other side of the state, a good six hours from Sevierville. The second possibility was Kevin Leib, another firebug who had a record for setting fires because he loved to watch them burn. But he'd been hired out by a guy who'd burned his own house down for the insurance money. Kevin was out on parole, his last-known address being Nashville, which was three to four hours away.

He called and left messages for both parole officers, requesting a call back. As it was Saturday, he doubted he'd hear from either of them until Monday.

But it was a start.

Linc worked for ninety minutes, before pushing the laptop aside. The chemical components he'd found at

Jayme's house and her car were not typical of Foley or Leib. Yet he wasn't willing to rule either of them out.

When he glanced over at Jayme, he found her scribbling in a notebook. She must have gotten it from her duffel because it looked like something a college student might use. He didn't have any of those types of notebooks sitting around.

"What are you working on?"

"Huh?" She looked up. "Oh, nothing really. I just had a new idea that I wanted to put in writing so I wouldn't forget."

"An idea for what?" Intrigued, he went over to the sofa. "Are you back in school?"

"No, it's just silly stories that I come up with." She closed the notebook as if to protect what she'd written from his prying eyes. "Nothing important."

"A diary?" He wondered if keeping a diary had helped her cope with everything she'd been through.

"No, a diary is something that really happened. I just make up stories." She set the notebook aside. "Did you find anything interesting?"

He wanted to ask what she thought of the Christian suspense but decided to let it go. After what she'd been through, pushing his faith on her probably wasn't smart. In fact, she was incredibly well adjusted considering what she'd endured.

What she'd overcome.

"Linc?" Jayme's voice broke into his thoughts.

"Yeah, as a matter of fact, I did. Come over here for a minute. I'd like to know if either of these guys looks familiar." He returned to the computer and brought both suspects' mug shots up on the screen.

Jayme took her time peering at one photo, then the

other. After a long silence, she reluctantly shook her head. "This guy"—she tapped Leib's photo—"looks a little familiar. But I can't say when or where I've seen him. The other guy is a complete stranger."

"Kevin Leib is an arsonist out on parole, currently living in Nashville."

"Maybe we should drive over to pay him a visit."

In a typical investigation, where he was working alone, he'd have done exactly that. But he wasn't keen on taking Jayme with him or leaving her home alone.

"I've got a call into his parole officer. Since you can't really ID him as someone who's been hanging around recently, it's better to go through official channels first." He minimized both mug shots. "I know you didn't recognize Terrance, but I'm still planning to place both of these guys as possible suspects in my report."

"I guess that's progress." The doubt in her tone belied her words.

"I know this seems to be moving at a snail's pace but trust the process. We'll find the person responsible."

"I trust you." Her gaze met his. "More than I trust anyone else. Well, other than Caitlyn."

"I'm honored," he said with somber sincerity. Easy to see that Jayme didn't trust easily. And he didn't blame her.

That she trusted anyone at all was a minor miracle.

Her phone beeped with an incoming text. She drew it from her pocket and smiled at the message. "Sounds like Caitlyn and Annette are having a great time."

It was tempting to ask when the last time Jayme had done something for fun, but he was afraid the answer might be never. "I'm glad to hear it."

She typed in a quick response, then glanced up at him.

"I should be mad at her for calling off work. But I'm relieved she's far away from here. Away from the danger."

"Hey." He reached out to cradle her scarred hand in his. "Try not to think about it, okay? If Kevin Leib is our guy, then he probably doesn't have his sights set on your sister."

"But if the Preacher is still alive . . ." She didn't continue the thought.

She didn't have to.

"Come on, let's find someplace to eat dinner." He stood and drew her up too. "How about I take you out to a restaurant you've never been to?"

She arched a brow. "That wouldn't be too difficult, I don't eat out at restaurants. And you've already succeeded in that mission. Our lunch today at the Red Mill was someplace I've never been."

"Okay, then we're going to try something a little nicer."

"Oh, no. I don't have anything nice to wear. This"—she waved at her jeans—"is as nice as it gets."

"You look fine." Better than fine, but he reminded himself not to go there. "Everything here is casual, even if the atmosphere is nicer. Do you like steak or seafood?"

"I like just about everything, especially food that hasn't been found in a garbage can." Her smile was wry. "I can't tell you how surprised I was to find the food pantry. I hadn't even known they'd existed."

When she made those types of statements, so casual like, they cut him off at the knees. To be that hungry, that desperate. He honestly couldn't imagine. He cleared his throat and tried not to let her know how much she affected him. "Okay, then let's try Sampson's Steak and Seafood. It's really great."

"Do you know that owner too?"

He winced. "Not on a first-name basis."

"Hmm. I take that to mean you do." She placed the Christian suspense book on top of her notebook, then reached for her purse. "You really don't have to keep feeding me like this. We could just as easily throw in a frozen pizza. I'm not that picky."

"I'd rather treat you to something nice." Not as a date but as a way to cheer up a friend.

She followed him outside, glancing around as he opened the car door for her. "Aren't you worried that the arsonist might find me here? I don't want anything to happen to you just because you're being extra nice to me."

The thought had occurred to him, but he'd dismissed it. "From what I can see, this guy is hitting places that are specific to you."

"I guess that's true."

The drive to Sampson's didn't take long. It was a Saturday night, and busy, but thankfully the wait wasn't too long. Once they were seated, she lifted her water glass and took a sip. "I don't even have to see the menu to know the food here is expensive."

"It's not that bad. And remember, I'm the one who chose the restaurant." He'd have given her the moon and all the stars in the sky if he could.

On the heels of that thought came the realization that he was slowly but surely letting this woman get too close. In a way that scared him.

He tried to conjure Gina's face and the beautiful image of Melody, his two-year-old daughter.

Melody was easy to recall, but Gina? He almost reached for his wallet to pull out the picture he carried.

Because the only woman he could see clearly was the pretty redhead sitting across from him.

JAYME HAD BEEN to three different restaurants with Linc. As much as she appreciated his willingness to spend his money on feeding her, she would have been more comfortable sitting at home and eating a frozen pizza.

The life Linc Quade lived was very different from hers. Eating out, buying books and keeping them to read whenever the mood struck. She couldn't imagine spending her money so frivolously.

She hadn't wanted to admit how much she was enjoying the suspense she'd taken from his bookshelf. There was a thread of faith woven through the story, but it was subtle rather than in your face.

It was also a little shocking to realize a book that even mentioned God and prayer was actually written by a New York Times Bestselling author. That meant there were a lot of people out there who'd read it. And loved it.

And maybe even believed in it.

Mind-boggling, to say the least.

Their server arrived and provided menus and rattled off a couple of the specials. Jayme tried not to show her ignorance about some of the menu items. She'd had steak, cooked badly, but had never tried swordfish or mahi-mahi. As predicted, everything was incredibly expensive.

Surely it would be cheaper to buy something from the grocery store and cook it?

"I'm going to have the swordfish," Linc declared. "What about you?"

"I—uh, don't know. I've never tried most of this stuff."

"Why not order the mahi-mahi, and we can share. If you like mine better, we'll swap." Linc smiled. "I'm sure you'll love it, though."

"Sounds good." She closed the menu. Really, how bad could it be?

"You know, if you don't like the book you picked out from my bookcase, you're welcome to try a different one."

"What makes you think I didn't like it?"

"Oh, well, because you stopped reading it to write in your notebook." He grimaced. "I just figured you got bored with the story."

"No, it's a good book, thanks. When I get certain ideas, I'm compelled to write them down so I don't forget." She didn't want him to ask about her stories. Her dream of being a published author someday was just that, a dream.

Something personal that no one could take away. Back when she lived with the Preacher, she'd often made up stories in her head as a way to escape the horror of her daily life. In her mind, she was often rescued by a handsome stranger.

Until the day she'd been forced to rescue herself.

Now her stories helped keep her busy, especially now that Caitlyn was moving on with her life.

"I'm glad to hear you like the book."

She tipped her head to the side. "Did you think I wouldn't?"

He flushed, and she wanted to laugh at his discomfort. "I wasn't sure."

"I admit it was surprising to read about characters who actually believe in God," she admitted. "But it would be silly to toss a book aside because they mention having faith."

"There's always something to learn from reading a book, even fiction."

Having casual conversation over dinner was a novelty for her. Especially since this was their second meal together in the same day. "You know all about me, so how about you tell me what you miss the most about being a firefighter?"

"The guys," he responded without hesitation. "Working as a team. My job now is rather lonely."

"Do you wish you could go back to being a firefighter?"

"No, I like being an investigator. And I don't miss the schedule."

She remembered he'd mentioned being on twenty-four, then off for forty-eight. "But you get called to arson fires in the middle of the night too."

"Yeah, but not as often as you'd think." He took a sip of his water. "The other downside to this job is that, thankfully, there aren't that many arson fires to investigate. Sometimes I get bored."

"I can understand that. My job can sometimes be a little mundane. I like taking care of patients, but there are always those who cause problems."

"Like Gary?"

"Exactly. Not everyone who comes to therapy is there to help themselves. Some come in with unrealistic expectations."

"Did you ever want to go on to become a physical therapist?"

"Not really. It's a long haul, and they expect you to have a doctorate these days." She shook her head. "The pay is not worth it."

"But what if paying for school wasn't an issue? I mean, what if you could do anything you wanted?"

I'd be a writer.

Thankfully, their meals arrived, saving her from answering. Linc reached across the table and took her hand. She wasn't sure why until he began to pray in a very low voice.

"Dear Lord, thank You for keeping Jayme safe all these years. And thank You for this food we are about to eat. We pray You continue guiding us on Your chosen path. Amen."

She didn't respond, mostly because her throat was too tight. She'd never in her life heard anyone pray out loud, and certainly no one other than Linc had ever included her.

"Dig in," he urged, not seeming to think anything was wrong. "I'm curious to know if you like the mahi-mahi."

She picked up her fork and took a bite. The tangy taste had her eyes widening in surprise. "Wow, it's really good."

"What, you were expecting dog food?"

"Of course not. But I never thought of fish having this kind of flavor." For someone who liked to write, she couldn't seem to come up with the words to describe it. Food was generally fuel, something she ate to keep up her strength. This was delicious. "I'm sure this is much better than your swordfish."

"Take a bite, see for yourself." He cut a small piece and put it on her plate.

"It's good," she admitted. "But I like mine better."

Linc laughed, the husky sound rippling over her in a way that made her long for something she couldn't have.

Him.

His phone rang. He frowned at the screen, then glanced at her. "I need to take this. Might be about the case."

"Go ahead."

Linc rose as he spoke into the phone. "This is Quade."

She wished she could hear the other side of the conversation, but Linc walked through the restaurant to go outside. For some reason, the secrecy jabbed deep.

What, he didn't trust her? She'd told him everything about her past, thinking he might open up more about his wife and daughter.

But he hadn't.

Whatever. This little interlude was just a temporary blip in both of their regular routines. A disruption that wouldn't last for long.

Or so she hoped.

Linc was a great host, falling over himself to make her feel welcome, but it wasn't easy for her to relax her guard in his space.

She continued eating her food, thinking his was growing colder by the minute. When he returned, she lifted a brow. "Good news?"

"That was Kevin Leib's parole officer. He was just filling me in on Kevin's progress." He took a bite of his swordfish. "I was hoping the guy was back to setting fires, but according to the parole officer, there haven't been any suspicious fires in Nashville over the past few weeks."

"How often does Kevin have to report in?"

"Weekly, although the parole officer has the right to ask him to come in at any time." Linc eyed her across the table. "If Leib doesn't report within the hour of being contacted, he'd be considered in violation of his parole and would be tossed back in jail."

"Wow." Jayme was glad she'd never been arrested. She'd been close, but thankfully, she had always been given the benefit of the doubt and released. "Harsh."

"They're out on parole rather than being in jail, so not so harsh," Linc said. "Anyway, this guy is going to request Kevin report in on Monday. I'll head over to meet with him, see what he knows about any of the fires here in Sevierville."

"I'd like to go with you to Nashville. It's not like I'll have to report in for work at the clinic, thanks to the fire." She sincerely hoped she wouldn't lose her job over the stupid firebomb. How long would it take them to repair the damage and replace any broken equipment?

Probably too long.

Linc reluctantly nodded. "Okay, you can tag along. But you can't say anything or be a part of the conversation with Kevin. You're a victim in these fires, you're not part of the investigation."

"Fine with me. I just want to see what Kevin looks like. Seeing his mug shot, there was something a little familiar about him."

"Could be you saw someone who strongly resembles him," Linc said.

"I know." She couldn't place him in any particular situation, so Linc's assumption was probably on target. But she wouldn't know that for sure unless she saw him up close and not wearing prison orange.

They ate the rest of their meal in silence. Jayme ate every last bite of her mahi-mahi to the point her stomach was uncomfortably full.

She should have saved half for a future meal. Yet she still had her leftover spaghetti and meatballs in Linc's fridge.

As Linc took care of the check, she excused herself to go to the restroom. When she emerged a few minutes later, Linc was standing nearby. "All set?"

"Yes." She led the way outside. The fall air was crisp and cool, and she lifted her face to soak in the breeze. Winter was lurking around the corner, bringing Caitlyn's graduation from her two years of college and then the holidays.

She wondered about the other foster kids. If they were still alive and doing well. At the time, splitting up had been the right decision.

But now, maybe because her future seemed rather empty, she'd been thinking more about the others. Wishing she could see them, check in with them. In fact, maybe she shouldn't ask a stranger to move in but rather extend the offer to one of the fosters. Once she found them.

She reached for her purse, then frowned. "Wait!" She spun back toward the restaurant. "I'm sorry, I need to go back inside. I left my purse hanging on the hook on the restroom door."

"That's fine, we're not in a rush." Linc turned to follow her back into the building.

She'd barely reached the door when a loud explosion rocked the earth, sending her flying off her feet and hitting the solid structure.

Linc hit her from behind, knocking the breath from her body. Sandwiched between Linc and the door, she tried to understand what just happened. Then the door opened, and Linc managed to pull her out of the way as customers streamed from the restaurant.

He wrapped his arms around her, sheltering her with his body. "Stay down," he whispered. Or maybe he wasn't speaking softly and she simply couldn't hear. Because all the sounds were muffled.

She managed to turn her head enough to see the source of the explosion. Flames blazed from the vehicle about thirty yards from where they'd been standing. A familiar black car.

Linc's SUV.

She blinked, hoping she was wrong. But she wasn't.

The arsonist had followed her long enough to know she was with Linc.

Targeting his car proved it.

CHAPTER EIGHT

Linc clutched Jayme close, sweeping his gaze over the area for the person responsible for blowing up his car, or for anyone who might have been injured. It must have been a relatively small bomb or the blast would have killed them.

Then again, if Jayme hadn't forgotten her purse in the restroom, they'd have been closer to the explosion.

This latest incident only reinforced his thought that this guy wasn't your typical arsonist. A firebug liked fire. Not necessarily planting bombs.

Sirens indicated help was on the way. He gingerly rose to his feet, drawing Jayme up too. Still, he kept his body in front of hers, just in case the assailant was still out there with another Molotov cocktail, or whatever device he'd used on his SUV.

"It's my fault you're involved in this . . ." Jayme's voice was low. "He must be following me to have seen us together."

"I'm glad I was here with you." He leaned down to press a chaste kiss to her temple. "We're safe, that's all that matters." He sent up a silent prayer, thanking God for watching over them again.

This attempt had been far too close.

"For how long?" Jayme's bitter tone made him wince. "Seriously, what is he going to blow up next?"

"We'll find a safe place to go." He couldn't deny she made a good point. If this guy continued his current escalation pattern, her house and his would be the next targets.

With a goal of killing Jayme.

The impact of that thought hit him with the force of an iron beam. This guy was using fire to scare Jayme before killing her.

Something Simon Penske a.k.a. the Preacher might do, if the guy was still alive.

Or maybe the perp was someone who knew her story? One of her foster siblings? He couldn't discount the possibility. Even Marco Edgar could have hired someone who'd uncovered the truth about Jayme's background. Enough to use it as a way to threaten her.

But out of all the suspects, he kept coming back to the Preacher. Seeing Simon and Ruth's obituary hadn't convinced him were truly dead. Well, one of them was, they had found human remains in the fire. But which one? Couldn't the ME say for sure if the remains were male or female? Maybe there just wasn't enough to tell.

From what he'd heard of Jayme's gut-wrenching story, he'd say the Preacher was someone who would save himself above all others. Even his wife.

According to Jayme, none of the foster kids had seen him get out of the house through the most logical exit, the doorway located farthest away from the fire. But he easily could have gone out a window in one of the bedrooms.

"I can try to get a loan to pay you back . . ."

"No." He tightened his arms around her. "Jayme, this is not your fault. The person who made the bomb and set it off is the one responsible. Besides, this is why I pay car insurance." His attempt to lighten the mood fell flat. "Please, don't worry about me. Let's just figure out where to go from here."

"That's just it." She rested her head against his chest for a long moment before pulling out of his arms. "No matter where I go, who I stay with, it's clear danger will follow. I refuse to put anyone in harm's way."

"I'm not leaving you alone, Jayme." He glanced over as the fire trucks and the police arrived. For the second time that day, he crossed over to meet up with the team.

"Same perp?" the captain asked.

"I think so." He scowled. "Only this time he went for more of an explosion rather than just tossing a firebomb through a window."

"Anyone hurt?"

"Not that I'm aware of." Although he looked again to make sure he hadn't missed seeing anyone who'd been hit from the explosion. "The blast knocked us off our feet, but we aren't hurt."

"Linc? I think there's a woman who has been hurt." Jayme abruptly rushed over to an area on the opposite side of the burning car.

He followed, hoping, praying the injury wasn't serious.

Jayme reached her first, dropping to her knees beside her. The older woman was leaning against the car, holding her head. "Hurts," the woman whispered.

"Let me see," Jayme gently removed the woman's hand. He used his phone flashlight app to brighten the area. "I see a bruise forming, but you'll need to go to the hospital for testing. I'm concerned you might have a concussion."

"Are you a nurse?" the dazed woman asked.

"No." Jayme glanced up at him. "Is the ambulance here? They should come and examine her."

He lifted his arm, waving the fire captain over. The ambulance crew arrived a moment later. The EMTs checked the woman over before placing her on the gurney and rolling her toward the ambulance.

Satisfied the woman would survive, he turned his attention to what was left of his SUV. The vehicle was still smoldering, but the fire had been quickly doused by the firefighters. Upon closer inspection, it appeared as if the origin of the damage was focused on the front passenger seat.

Where Jayme would have been sitting.

He rubbed the back of his neck, trying to figure out how the bomber had gotten the device into his car. The windows were shattered, so he couldn't tell if the passenger window had been somehow cut open or if the bomb had been sitting beneath the seat for the past few hours. The idea of Jayme sitting on top of a bomb that could have gone off at any time made him feel sick. Then again, if that was truly the case, then the perp could have hit the trigger to blow them up while they were driving.

Or when they'd parked outside the restaurant.

No, he felt certain it had to have been placed while they'd been inside the restaurant. He reviewed the timeline in his head. The guy must have seen them approaching the car, hit the trigger a second or two earlier than he'd intended at the exact same time he and Jayme had turned to go back inside to retrieve her purse.

God had saved them.

"I hope her concussion isn't too bad." Jayme's comment interrupted his thoughts. "I feel awful enough knowing your car has been destroyed. If that woman had been killed . . ."

"Again, this isn't your fault. You're a victim here, just like that woman." He cupped her shoulders in his hands. "Please stop carrying the responsibility for this arsonist's actions on your shoulders. He's the criminal, not you."

"In my head I know you're right. But in my heart?" She shook her head. "I can't help but feel guilty."

"For what? Surviving a fire thirteen years ago? For escaping an abusive foster home? For creating a new life for yourself and your younger sister?" He tried not to let his frustration show. "You're a woman to admire; there's nothing at all for you to feel guilty about." He blew out a heavy sigh and gentled his tone. "Jayme, I really wish you could put your faith and trust in God. To know that He is watching over us and has a plan for us."

She opened her mouth as if she were going to say something but then hesitated. "I'm amazed you can say that after the tragic way you lost your wife and daughter."

"It hasn't been easy. There were months when I was so angry at God for what He'd done. But returning to church helped, and slowly, over time, my faith grew stronger. I think what helped me through the most was knowing that Gina and Melody are in a better place. That they're in heaven together and with God."

Jayme's gaze clung to his as she slowly nodded. "I have to admit that sounds really nice. We didn't hear anything from the Preacher about heaven."

"Maybe because he's the devil and has no knowledge of what God has in store for those of us who believe in Him." He shifted, feeling a bit uncomfortable in his role as pastor. "From what you've described? That man never ever spoke God's word. He told lies, upon lies, upon lies."

"Like the devil," she whispered.

"Yes, exactly like the devil." He drew her into his arms. "I'm going to do everything in my power to keep you safe. And we're going to find the person who is trying to hurt you."

A tremulous smile tipped the corners of her mouth. "I believe in you, Linc. More than I've ever trusted anyone."

Her words humbled him, and he sent up a prayer asking for the strength he'd need to make good on his promise. "Thank you."

"No, thank you." She went up on her tiptoes and kissed him. Their lips brushed, then held. As before, sparks flew as he deepened the kiss.

He couldn't seem to get enough of her sweet taste. Of her warmth and generous spirit.

The kiss was over far too soon.

"Sorry, I just needed to be held for a moment." Jayme pulled away from him and drew her hand through her hair. "Thanks for being such a great friend."

"Anytime." He hoped she didn't notice how much of a punch her kiss had packed. He cleared his throat, trying to sound normal, as if another bomb hadn't gone off in the region of his chest. "Give me a few minutes to talk to the firefighters, then I'll get you out of here."

"Okay. I'll get my purse from the restroom." She lightly touched his arm before turning away.

He sucked in a quick breath in an attempt to clear his head. Linc glanced over to where the firefighters were gathered and headed toward them. He couldn't bear the thought of failing Jayme. The night of the storm, when his wife and daughter had been sideswiped by a semitruck and killed, there hadn't been anything he could have done to change the outcome. He'd been working his twenty-four-hour shift and hadn't even known about Gina's last-minute road trip to visit her parents in Memphis.

A decision followed by a freak accident that had cost him his family.

This was different. Jayme was being stalked by someone who wanted her to relive the fire she'd escaped thirteen years ago. A man who made attempts against her right under Linc's nose. He felt compelled to keep Jayme safe.

To protect her.

With his own life, if necessary.

Because this might be the reason God had changed the course of his life. To be here in this moment to shield Jayme.

A calling he would not refuse or ignore.

***

JAYME DUCKED into the restaurant bathroom to grab her purse, then stood outside and watched Linc talking to the firefighters on scene, doing her best to ignore that kiss. She really needed to get her impulses under control. The poor man had made it clear he'd never love anyone but his wife and daughter.

So why on earth did she keep throwing herself at him?

It needed to stop. Especially since she didn't need more rejection in her life.

Granted, Linc was too nice to make it that obvious. No, he'd let her kiss him, even though he didn't want anything more than friendship.

Her brain must be misfiring for some reason. She normally avoided romantic entanglements. The moment her former boyfriend had left because she'd refused to sleep with him and apparently kept herself aloof, Jayme remembered thinking to herself, *Thank goodness he's gone.*

Her gaze returned to the charred frame of Linc's car. If Eli had still been in the picture, one incident like this would have had the guy running away from her as fast and furious as possible.

No way would he have offered to help her out, much less attempt to keep her safe.

She drifted closer to Linc and the firefighters, catching parts of their conversation through the faint ringing in her ears.

". . . the passenger seat," Linc was saying. "I want the SUV towed to the garage so I can examine it more closely."

She turned to look back at the SUV. Passenger seat? Did Linc believe that to be the location from where the bomb went off?

That side of the car did look more damaged than the driver's side. Or maybe that was just her imagination spinning out of control.

"Ms. Weston?" Jayme glanced at the police officer coming toward her. "I need your statement."

Jayme had never spoken to as many cops in her entire life as she had over the past two days. "Of course."

The cop's name tag identified him as Officer Hill. He drew her away from the others so they could speak privately. Her statement didn't take long considering she had been on her way back inside the restaurant to get her purse when the explosion had taken place.

Still, he asked several follow-up questions, repeats of what she'd been asked after earlier incidents. It was tempting to ask Officer Hill to read the other reports, but she managed to refrain.

"I'm sorry, I don't have any idea who is behind all of this." She glanced over Hill's shoulder to see Linc heading over to join them. "As I told the previous officers earlier today and yesterday, I don't have enemies. Marco Edgar is the only person that was upset with me, and that was six years ago."

"Marco Edgar?" Hill looked excited to have a potential suspect.

"He hasn't left California," Linc said, ruthlessly bursting the cop's bubble. "I've looked at two possible arsonists for hire, Terrance Foley and Kevin Leib. Leib is recently on parole and has an address in Nashville. Foley is supposedly living in Memphis."

Officer Hill wrote the names down. "We can check with the local cops in those areas, see if they have anything on either of these guys."

"Thanks." Linc nodded. "I've contacted their respective parole officers too. I pray we learn something helpful soon."

"I need your statement too, Mr. Quade." Hill glanced at Jayme. "If you'd give us a moment alone?"

She nodded and moved away, knowing by now this was all part of the police routine. They didn't want witnesses to compare stories.

The cool night breeze picked up, making her shiver. She watched as patrons came out of the restaurant in droves, clearly unwilling to stick around the scene of an explosion, and wondered how much business Sampson's lost tonight because of the car bomb.

Guilt pressed heavily against the center of her chest. Linc had told her several times that none of this was her fault, yet if she and Linc hadn't come for dinner tonight, Sampson's wouldn't be suffering.

Her hair whipped over her face. As she pushed it back, a flash of movement caught her eye. A figure wearing a black coat and a black stocking hat was leaving the restaurant parking lot on foot.

A customer? Somehow, she didn't think so. The way he kept his head down made it seem as if he was avoiding eye contact. Remembering what Linc had said about firebugs sticking around to watch a fire burn had her following the guy. She picked up her pace, moving quietly in an effort to get a better look at him.

If she could just see his face . . .

At that exact moment, he turned just enough to glance over his shoulder. She was still too far away to see his features with any clarity, especially in the darkness, but he must have recognized her because he began to run.

Without hesitation, she broke into a run too. "Hey! You! Stop!" she shouted as loud as possible, hoping the cops around the area would notice.

The guy darted around a corner. She sprinted toward it, but when she reached the street, it was too dark to see anything.

He was gone.

"Jayme!" Linc's panicked shout had her turning around. He was rushing toward her, a wild look in his eyes. "Are you okay?"

"No. I lost him." She reined in her temper with an effort. "I was hoping the police would pick up the chase."

"Lost who?" He slowed to a stop, his gaze searching hers. "Who were you running after?"

"The man in black." She put her hands on her hips. "Didn't you see him?"

"No. I only saw you running, then yelling out." He looked over her shoulder at the street beyond. "What did he look like?"

"Medium height and build, dressed in black, including a stocking cap on his head. I had the impression he had dark hair beneath, but I could be wrong. I only caught a brief glimpse of his face."

"What's going on?" Officer Hill asked as he joined them.

Jayme bit back a flash of impatience as she repeated what she'd seen. At this point, it didn't matter. The guy was long gone.

"Was the guy older or younger?" Linc asked.

"Maybe in his late forties? Not young, but not that old." She was convinced the guy in black wasn't the Preacher. If the Preacher had survived the fire, he'd probably be scarred and disfigured. Likely handicapped in some way too. Hardly in a position to be sprinting away from the scene of a crime. "He was physically fit based on how fast he was moving."

And how quickly he'd disappeared from sight.

An innocent bystander? A petty crook looking to take advantage of the chaos outside the restaurant? Or the arsonist?

She had no clue.

"Do you need anything else, Officer Hill?" Linc asked. "I'd like to get Ms. Weston someplace safe."

"That's fine. Please call the station if you think of anything else," Hill said.

"We will." Linc took her hand and walked back toward the section of the parking lot that had streetlights. "I'm calling a rideshare."

She nodded, battling another wave of guilt. A wave of exhaustion hit hard, and she recognized the adrenaline crash. When the white sedan pulled up, she gratefully climbed inside.

Linc gave the driver the name of a chain hotel, much

more upscale than the Shady Lane. The price would be exorbitant, but she couldn't bring herself to complain.

She wasn't in the mood to battle cockroaches or bedbugs.

Neither of them spoke as the rideshare driver made his way to the hotel. The traffic was nonexistent, so it didn't take long. She wanted to request a detour to Linc's house to get her things but told herself to get over it.

One night without her duffel bag wouldn't kill her. This was the type of hotel that would offer basic toiletries too.

"We'd like two connecting rooms, please," Linc told the clerk. He handed over his credit card and ID. "On the first floor if possible."

"Of course, that won't be a problem, Mr. Quade." The cheery clerk quickly entered Linc's information into the computer, then handed him his ID and credit card back. "Is there anything else you need?"

"A toothbrush," she and Linc said at the same time. Then they both laughed.

It felt good to laugh, even over something silly. Better than crying.

After they'd each been given their keys, toothbrushes, toothpaste, and a small map to show them to their rooms, they headed down the side hallway. Linc stopped outside the business suite.

"I want you to look at something." He drew her into the room and powered up the closest computer. After a few minutes, he had the two mug shots of the arson-for-hire suspects on the screen. "Either of these two guys the one you followed?"

She took a moment to bring the brief memory of the man's face to her mind. It was difficult because it had all happened so fast. "Terrance Foley has lighter hair, I don't think he was the runner. Kevin is a possibility. His hair is dark, and he's the approximate age." She shrugged help-lessly. "I just can't say for sure. And honestly, he may not have been the arsonist."

"I know." He clicked out of the photos and shut off the computer. "I'll rent a car first thing tomorrow morning. We'll need one to get to get around and to drive to Nashville to visit Kevin's parole officer on Monday."

"Are you sure that's a good idea? What if this guy torches that one too?"

"I don't think he followed us here to the hotel." Linc rested his hand in the small of her back as they walked down the hall to their side-by-side rooms. "We'll just have to find a way to stay off his radar."

She pulled out her key and unlocked her door. "It's not like Sevierville is a very large city. Someone determined to find us would start with this type of hotel."

"I'm not staying at the Shady Lane, and neither are you." Linc opened his door. "I need you to unlock your side of the connecting door, okay?"

"Okay." She entered the room, set the toothbrush and toothpaste on the bathroom counter, then went over to open the connecting door. Turning back, she could hardly believe she would be sleeping here.

It was nicer than any place she'd ever stayed in. And that included her house.

"Hey, are you all right?"

She turned to face Linc. "How can I complain about a place like this?"

He frowned. "It's nothing fancy."

It was to her, but she let it go. "I—uh, probably should get some sleep. It's been an incredibly long day."

"It has. I just wanted to be sure you weren't hurt when

that bomb exploded." His intense gaze raked over her. "I slammed into you pretty hard."

"I might have a few bruises, nothing more." She unconsciously rubbed her scarred hand. "I'm fine."

"Jayme." He sighed and ran his fingers through his short blond hair. "Can we talk?"

Weren't they talking already? But then she realized they were both standing awkwardly near the connecting door. "Sure." She went over to sit in the chair. He dropped down onto the edge of the bed.

"I'd like you to consider going into a safe house for the next week."

His blunt statement made her recoil backward in surprise. "What kind of safe house?"

"One that is set up by the local police or maybe even the Feds." He stared down at his hands before meeting her gaze. "I need you to be safe while I continue investigating these fires. And keeping you with me tonight almost got you killed."

"Both of us killed," she corrected.

"But you're the target, Jayme. I'm just icing on the cake for this guy." He shifted and added, "I can't investigate this arsonist as thoroughly as I need to if I'm constantly watching over you."

Ouch. That stung, more than it should.

"I understand." She tried to sound positive, despite the fact that she didn't like the idea. Being pushed off on strangers felt a bit like how she'd moved through the foster system, ending up with the Preacher.

Not that this was the same thing by any stretch of the imagination. She wasn't paranoid enough to believe that the police or whoever was assigned to protect her would take advantage of the situation.

Still, she knew Linc. Felt comfortable with him. And if she were completely honest with herself, she didn't want to leave him.

Which was her problem, not his.

"After we pick up the rental car, I'll make some arrangements for you." Linc's smile seemed forced. "The sooner you're safe, the sooner I can catch this guy."

"I know." She lifted her chin. "That's the most important thing. I appreciate your efforts, Linc."

"I . . . wish I'd been able to do more." His dark eyes were mesmerizing to the point she had to force herself to look away. "I won't fail you, Jayme."

"I know you won't." She rose and edged around him. "Good night, Linc. I'm sure tomorrow will be another busy day."

"Good night." He brushed past her on the way to the connecting door. It took every ounce of self-control she possessed not to reach out and beg him to hold her.

Since when was she so needy? Clingy? Unsettled?

Since never.

Jayme crossed her arms over her chest and waited for Linc to retreat into his room. He left his side of the door open an inch, so she did the same. Then she cleaned up in the bathroom and used the toothbrush and toothpaste before crawling into bed.

Yet despite the soft mattress and plush comforter, she tossed and turned, unable to get comfortable.

Even though she wasn't a little kid anymore, she still felt much like she had the night before another move to yet another foster home.

Full of worry and dread of what the following day would bring.

CHAPTER NINE

Linc knew sending Jayme to a safe house was the right thing to do. So why was he having second thoughts? Why did everything inside of him rebel at the idea of dropping her off with strangers and going back to his investigation?

His head was a jumbled mess of emotion, which only proved that putting Jayme in a safe house was the right thing to do. For both of them.

But the flicker of uncertainty in her gaze before she'd agreed ate at him.

After a rough night, he hit the shower and mentally listed the things he needed to accomplish, starting with obtaining a rental car. Normally on Sundays he attended church, but that wouldn't be possible today.

God would understand and continue to keep him safe.

Jayme too.

When Linc emerged from the bathroom, he smelled coffee. Following his nose, he opened the connecting door between their rooms.

Jayme's hair was damp from a recent shower. She was curled in the chair, sipping coffee. She didn't smile, only gave a brief nod. "Good morning. I heard you were up, so I made coffee for you."

"Thanks." Her words were nice, but her expression could have been carved from granite. He felt a bit like he was navigating a minefield. "How did you sleep?"

She shrugged. "Strange bed."

Okay, now he was certain she was upset with him. About the safe house? Last night she'd agreed to go. "Did you change your mind?"

She glanced away. "I wasn't aware I had that option."

He set his coffee aside and moved over to sit across from her. "Jayme, you know my only goal here is to keep you safe."

"I know." Her blue gaze was somber. "That's what the social workers always said before moving me from one foster home to the next. Only they hadn't proved to be safe at all. Especially not when we'd ended up with the Preacher."

The puzzle pieces clicked into place. "I'm sorry, Jayme. I didn't intend to make you feel like I was abandoning you."

"You're not." She took another sip of her coffee. "Don't worry about me, I'll be fine."

She wasn't, and he knew it. Yet he couldn't figure out a way to keep her with him while he continued investigating these incidents, especially at the rate they were occurring.

This particular assailant was proving to be relentless. And Linc knew the attacks would continue unless he found a way to stop them.

He desperately needed a break in the case. A clue that would help identify who was behind these attacks. And for that, he needed to stay focused, to examine each of the crime scenes for potential links to other known arsonists.

All of which made him steel his resolve. Despite what

he secretly wanted, placing Jayme in a safe house was the right thing to do.

"I need to make a few phone calls, then we'll get something to eat." He rose. "Give me fifteen minutes or so."

"That's fine. I'll be ready to go when you are." Her voice was steady. She remained curled up in the chair, looking toward the window that faced the Smoky Mountains.

He hated the way she'd withdrawn from him. The previous camaraderie he'd enjoyed seemed to have vanished.

For good? His gut clenched as he moved into his room.

He secured a rental car first, then made a call to Captain Barstow within the Sevierville Police Department.

"Barstow," he answered curtly.

"Captain, this is Linc Quade. Did you hear about the car bomb last night at Sampson's?"

"I did, this creep is escalating faster than we can keep up," Barstow admitted. "You and Ms. Weston are okay, though, right?"

"We are. But I need your help in getting Ms. Weston into a safe house as soon as possible." He stared out the hotel room window. "Based on the fact that my SUV was targeted, I think it's clear she can't stay at her house or mine."

"Where are you now?" Barstow asked.

"A hotel." He rose and paced the length of the room. "What do you think? Should we keep her here? Are you able to free up a cop to stand outside her door? Or do you have another place we can use?"

"Linc, you know I'd love to help you out as I've seen what this joker is doing, but I don't have the budget to place a uniform on her door twenty-four seven."

"What if I foot the bill?" Linc figured he could take a

second mortgage out on his house if needed. "I don't want to hire a security guard, I need an actual cop. Someone who knows how a criminal's mind works. This arsonist is determined to kill her."

There was a moment of silence before Barstow said, "I'll give you the names of several guys who are always looking for extra money. You'll have to pay them directly, though. I can't get in the middle of this."

"I would appreciate that. Can you give them my number and ask them to call me ASAP? And as a cop, what do you think about keeping her here or in a house somewhere?"

"There are pros and cons to both," Barstow said. "The house would be easier to protect from strangers, and to escape from if needed. The hotel is a public place, so there's no easy way to keep an eye on who is coming or going. But keeping her locked in her room would solve that problem. I assume you aren't looking to use her as bait to draw this arsonist out of hiding."

"No!" The suggestion caused his blood pressure to spike. "She's not bait, and honestly, I can't keep her locked in a room either." No way would he make her feel like she was back in the Preacher's cellar. "I'll find a house to use temporarily. I think she'll want to have a way to escape if needed."

"Okay, I'll make a few calls. Stay in touch."

"Thanks, Captain." Linc glanced at his watch and took a few minutes to look for rental homes available in the area. He found a small cabin nestled in the woods that would be easy to protect.

He went over to knock at the connecting room door. Jayme's side was still open, so he poked his head in. "Jayme?

Will you take a look at this place and let me know what you think?"

Her smile didn't quite reach her eyes. "Sure."

"If you don't like it, just tell me. I'll find something else." He showed her the cabin on his phone. "Is it too much like the one you stayed in with the Preacher?"

She swiped at the screen to view the various pictures. "It's very nice, and no, it isn't at all like being with the Preacher." She met his gaze as she handed back his phone. "I love the woods; it helped us escape."

"Are you absolutely sure you don't mind staying there? I don't want to upset you more than I already have."

"I'm not upset," she protested.

"Yeah, you are. I get why you're feeling that way; after all, I told you I would keep you safe." He sighed. "And that's still my goal, Jayme. I promise that your safety is my top priority. But I also need to find this guy, which means going back to the PT clinic to sift through the debris and then heading over to the garage to examine the damage to my vehicle. Stuff that will take up most of my day, and maybe into tomorrow."

"I understand, and I do appreciate your help." Her gaze was solemn. "But I'm worried about Caitlyn. She and Annette should be returning to Sevierville sometime today. I'd like them to join me at the cabin."

"Done." He would have moved the Earth's axis for her if he could have. He took a moment to book the cabin via his phone. "I need to pick up my rental car. We'll grab something to eat along the way before heading to the cabin. I'll wait with you there until the officer is able to relieve me."

"I'm ready." She turned to pick up her purse from the chair. He frowned when he noticed she'd made the bed but held his tongue, unwilling to shatter the fragile truce shimmering between them.

Hopefully, the maid would figure it out.

He left a tip on the bed before following Jayme out of the room and into the hall. Outside, he used his phone to obtain a rideshare.

"I need my power cord for my phone," Jayme said. "I'm not sure about your battery life, but I'm down to twenty percent, and I need to be able to talk to Caitlyn."

"Okay, I'll take care of it." Linc considered their options. He could swing by his place after dropping her off at the cabin to get her things. Or they could stop at a store. Although he'd need his power cord too.

And a change of clothes.

The rental car was another SUV, dark blue instead of black. An hour later, he pulled up in front of the cabin, feeling good that the rear part of the building was nestled close to the hillside. No one would be able to sneak up that way, they'd be forced to come in from the front.

"Oh, look. A hot tub. Too bad I didn't bring a bathing suit." Jayme's dry tone indicated she was joking.

"Maybe next time." He walked up to the door and punched in the code on the lockbox to access the key. Inside, the cabin smelled like lemons as if it had been recently cleaned. "I hope this works for you."

"Looks great." Difficult to tell if she was being sincere. "Thanks."

He wished he could do more, but he had to be satisfied with knowing Officer Rainer would be there soon. He'd already paid the young man using an online banking website.

"Books!" This time, there was no denying the excitement in Jayme's tone as she spied the bookshelves flanking the fireplace. She hurried over to examine them. When he remembered the notebook she'd used at his house, he mentally added that to the list of items he'd need to pick up for her.

Devon Rainer arrived five minutes later. Linc introduced the young, and annoyingly handsome, cop to Jayme. "Nice to meet you," Devon drawled.

Linc forced a smile. "I'll be here to relieve you at nine o'clock tonight." His efforts to cover the night shift had been futile. "Call me if you need something before then."

"Will do," Devon agreed. "I'm sure the most difficult thing we'll face today is boredom."

"Speak for yourself," Jayme piped up. "I've got books to read."

Devon looked a bit disappointed at her statement, which made Linc want to smile. "I'll be back with some additional things, okay?"

"Okay." Devon strolled over to the kitchen table. He was dressed in casual clothes, since he wasn't on police duty, but thankfully he carried his sidearm on his belt holster.

Linc left the cabin, praying the officer wouldn't have to use it.

JAYME DID her best to lose herself in her book, but it wasn't easy. The hired cop was grating on her nerves with his constant fidgeting. How on earth did he manage the simple task of patrolling the streets? There wasn't that much crime in Sevierville, there must be times when it was slow.

Linc had returned with her duffel bag, phone cord, and

her notebook, along with basic easy-to-fix food. When Linc had left for the second time, it was all she could do not to beg him to stay.

Hence, her desire to lose herself in her book.

She had to give Devon credit for taking his duty seriously. He walked around the outside of the property every thirty minutes. She felt safe enough in the cabin that would have been quaint under different circumstances. There was no way the arsonist would have been able to follow them there. But she still wasn't thrilled with the arrangements.

And if Devon interrupted her with inane chitchat one more time, she was going to seriously lose it.

"Hey, Jayme, are you hungry?" Devon was looking through the food Linc had stored in the refrigerator. "Looks like we have mixings for sandwiches here."

She bit her lip to prevent herself from snapping. "Help yourself. I'll grab something later."

"Maybe we should check out that hot tub." He winked at her from across the kitchen. "Could be fun."

"No thank you." Her phone rang, and she practically pounced on it in relief. "Caitlyn, are you on your way home?"

"Soon, I just got your message." Her sister sounded distracted. "What is all this about a safe house? Annette and I have classes tomorrow morning."

"But not until ten, right?" She knew full well her night-owl sister hadn't taken any early classes. "I'll make sure you and Annette get to school on time."

"Jayme, is this really necessary? We'd rather head to the apartment."

"Please don't do that," Jayme pleaded. "I've been in danger for the past two days. I wouldn't ask you to do this if it wasn't important."

"What kind of danger? Are you okay?" Caitlyn's voice held concern.

"I'm fine, but only because I've had help." She swallowed hard, knowing it was ridiculous to miss Linc, a man she hadn't known two days ago. "I'll give you directions to the cabin, let's at least talk things through before you make any rash decisions, okay?"

"Fine," Caitlyn sighed. "Go ahead and give me the address." Caitlyn's resigned tone made her feel better. Her sister might be irritated, but she wouldn't ignore the threat of danger.

Tension eased from her shoulders after her brief conversation with Caitlyn. Knowing her sister would be safe was a relief.

Now if Devon could only morph himself into someone with a better personality, she'd be even better.

When he took another walk outside, she made a quick sandwich. The kid was nice, but he was acting a bit too flirty for her peace of mind. Caitlyn was only twenty-two and had long blonde hair and beautiful blue eyes. If he continued with that attitude toward her sister, she might have to resort to drastic measures to get his attention.

The rest of the afternoon passed with excruciating slowness. She finished her book and wrote some notes about the plot of a new story that had been swirling around in her mind. Not that she wasn't living a suspense story in real life.

By five o'clock, she was concerned something had happened to her sister. She called, but Caitlyn didn't pick up.

It was her turn to pace the cabin, glancing constantly outside, hoping to see her sister's car pulling in. Even if the girls had gotten lost or stopped for food, they should have been here by now.

She eyed Devon's rusty pickup truck. His keys weren't sitting out, or she'd have already made a run for it.

Frustrated, she called Linc. He answered quickly. "Jayme? You okay?"

"No. Caitlyn should have been here two hours ago. She's not answering her phone, and I'm worried something has happened to her."

"Hang on a minute." She heard the muffled sounds of a conversation. "Okay, I'm finished here at the physical therapy building. I'll head over to the apartment to see if her car is there. A dark gray Honda, right?"

"Right." She let out a breath. "Okay, thanks. Call me back as soon as you can."

"I will. Try to stay calm, I'm sure she just stopped there to get her things."

Yeah, that's exactly what Jayme was afraid of. She gripped her phone tightly and continued her pacing.

What if the arsonist was hanging around Caitlyn's apartment because she was out of his reach? She'd done her best to protect Caitlyn from the harsh realities of living on the streets, but that may work against her now.

Would Caitlyn recognize a potentially dangerous man? Jayme was wired to be suspicious of everyone, but Caitlyn tended to be friendly and outgoing, even with strangers.

The way most young people were.

Fear gripped her tightly by the throat, making it difficult to breathe. She sank onto the sofa and bowed her head, hoping Caitlyn wasn't hurt.

Please, God, keep her safe!

The unbidden prayer slipped through her mind before she could think about it. And surprisingly, it brought a sense of peace.

"Jayme? You okay?"

She lifted her head. "I will be. Linc is going to see if he can find my sister and her friend. They should have been here by now."

Devon nodded. "I'd head out to look for them myself, but I promised Linc I wouldn't leave you alone."

Again, she couldn't fault the way he took his job seriously. "She drives a dark gray Honda, in case you notice one passing by."

"I'll keep a lookout for it." He glanced toward the fridge. "I was thinking of tossing in a frozen pizza for dinner. You interested?"

"Yeah, sure." Her stomach was so knotted up there was no way she'd be able to eat, but cooking the pizza would keep him busy.

And if Caitlyn did show up, she loved pizza.

Not if, when, she silently corrected. When Caitlyn and Annette showed up, they'd likely be hungry.

Her phone rang, and she gratefully answered Linc's call. "Did you find them?"

"Yes, they're here at the apartment." He sounded a bit tense, and she imagined the conversation hadn't gone well. "They're packing their stuff now. Apparently, your sister's phone battery died."

"Put her on, please." Jayme waited until she heard her sister's voice. "Caitlyn, what part of being in danger didn't you understand?"

"Hey, you didn't tell me that someone actually blew up your car," she said defensively. "I made sure we weren't followed, and we came in through the back door."

"But why did you go to the apartment at all?" Jayme asked. "I asked you to come straight here."

"We needed clean clothes to wear, and it only took us a

few minutes. Or would have if your guy friend hadn't tracked us down."

She loved her sister, she really did, but it wasn't easy to hang on to her temper. "There's a washer and dryer here. But never mind, just get over here as soon as possible."

"We will. Sorry, sis." At least Caitlyn sounded contrite.

"Jayme?" Linc had taken the phone. "I'll follow them to the cabin, okay?"

"Okay, thanks, Linc. I'll throw in another pizza for them. Devon ate most of the one he made."

"See you soon," Linc said before disconnecting from the line.

She slid her phone into her pocket, those three words brightening her day more than they should. It was ridiculous for her to have missed Linc in a measly eight-hour period of time.

These feelings she had for him were becoming a problem. The hero in the story she was writing had changed to the point that he looked just like Linc.

Fifteen minutes later, Caitlyn, Annette, and Linc arrived. She'd put two more pizzas in the oven just in case Linc was hungry too.

"Jayme, I'm so sorry about your car." Caitlyn came over to give her a big hug. "And I'm sorry we worried you. Linc filled us in on what's been happening."

"I'm glad you're here now." She glanced over Caitlyn's shoulder to find Linc. "Thanks for dropping everything to check on her."

"It's not a problem. Actually, I'm finished with investigating the two recent scenes," Linc admitted. "Devon, if you'd like to head home, I can take over from here."

"You just want to keep all the pretty girls for yourself,"

Devon joked, eyeing Caitlyn and Annette. "I can return tomorrow morning if needed."

"That would be great, thanks." Linc slapped the young officer on the shoulder. "I really appreciate your willingness to keep these women *safe*." The added emphasis on the last word wasn't lost on Devon. He may not be the sharpest knife in the drawer, but he understood a reprimand when he heard one.

"Yes, sir." Devon bobbed his head toward her. "Good night, Ms. Jayme."

Oh, so now she was Ms. Jayme? She smiled wryly. "Good night, Devon."

Linc locked the door behind him, then turned toward her. "Please tell me he didn't act too badly."

"He was mostly fine." She shrugged off her annoyance; after all, it wasn't Devon's fault she hadn't liked him.

Having Linc around relaxed her. Scary, but true. She donned quilted oven mitts and pulled the pizzas out. Caitlyn jumped in to set the table.

"It's my fault, Jayme," Annette said. "I'm the one who convinced Caitlyn to stop at the apartment."

"No, I should have insisted on coming straight here," Caitlyn countered. "I . . . should have known Jayme wasn't overreacting."

"I wasn't, but everything is fine now, right?" Jayme sliced the pizzas and set them in the center of the table. She dropped into the chair across from Linc, then folded her hands. "I know you'd like to pray."

"I would," Linc agreed. Caitlyn and Annette looked at each other in surprise but didn't say anything. "Dear Lord, we thank You for this food, for this safe place to stay, and for bringing Caitlyn and Annette home. Please continue guiding us on Your path. Amen."

"Amen," Jayme echoed.

Linc's eyes widened at her participation in his prayer, and when he smiled, she could feel herself blush. Not good with Caitlyn sitting right beside her.

Thankfully, the girls chatted about their trip to Nashville throughout the meal. When they were finished, Linc suggested the girls clean up, and both of them readily agreed.

"That was slick," she said in an undertone.

"Tell me the truth, do I need to knock a few of Devon's teeth out?" Linc asked.

She laughed for the first time in what seemed like forever. Somehow, she couldn't seem to stay mad at Linc. Even when she'd resented the fact that he'd exiled her to the cabin with Devon. "If I say yes, will you stay here instead?"

There was a moment of hesitation, as if he wasn't sure if she was joking. But then he smiled ruefully. "It wasn't easy for me to leave you here, Jayme. And to be honest, the day felt like a waste of time. There isn't enough of a link between these incidents from an arson perspective to say they were done by the same man." He shook his head. "I'm hoping that talking to Kevin Leib tomorrow will help."

All humor faded from her face. "And if it doesn't?"

"I don't know." His expression was full of frustration. "It's horrible to think that we might have to wait and see when and where he strikes next."

"Yeah, that's not good." She suppressed a sigh. "Thanks for being honest with me."

"Always." His low, husky voice made her remember the heat of their kisses.

Good thing the girls were here as a distraction. Which reminded her. "The girls need to go to class tomorrow at ten o'clock. I'd rather they not be alone."

"Ten o'clock, huh?" He grimaced and nodded. "I'll be on the road to Nashville, but Devon can drive them. You'll need to tag along."

"In his pickup truck? Or with you?" She held his gaze. "You said I could meet this arson suspect, right?"

"Yes. Okay, you and I will head to Nashville, and Devon can act as a bodyguard for Caitlyn and Annette." He glanced over to where they were finishing the dishes. "Girls? I want you to let me know if Officer Rainer steps out of line."

"You mean Devon?" Caitlyn asked as Annette giggled. "Don't worry, I'm sure he'll be a gentleman."

"He better be," Linc muttered.

The dark clouds made the hour seem later than it was. Both girls were exhausted from their trip, so they went to bed early. Jayme yawned, thinking it would be prudent to do the same.

"You sure you're okay on the sofa?" She thought it looked far too short for his frame.

"I'll be fine. I'm going to be up every few hours to check things out anyway."

She nodded. "Good night, then."

"Good night, Jayme."

She fell asleep quickly, maybe because of Linc's reassuring presence nearby, but awoke with a jolt to the sound of shattering glass.

"Jayme! Caitlyn! Annette!" Linc shouted loudly. "Hurry!"

She pulled on her shoes and sweater, then ran into the main living room to grab her purse. She gaped in surprise when she saw the broken window and fire sprouting from the center of the sofa.

The arsonist had found them!

CHAPTER TEN

My fault. This was all my fault!

Linc grabbed a quilt and tossed it over the burning sofa, even as he continued shouting for the girls to get up. Jayme rushed over to the kitchen, grabbed a large saucepan, and filled it with water. She tossed it onto the quilt, which helped tamp down the flames.

It was a temporary tactic at best, but enough to provide extra time for them to get out of there. Caitlyn and Annette stumbled from the bedroom.

"What's going on?" Annette asked.

"Fire!" Caitlyn shouted. "We need to get out of here!"

Sensing her panic, he quickly hustled them toward the door. "We're okay, but I need you to stay behind me." Linc wasn't sure if the arsonist was outside waiting for them to emerge from the burning cabin or if he was watching from afar. "Go straight to my SUV and get in, understand?"

"Yes, come on, Caitlyn. Annette." Jayme's face was pale in the darkness. "Follow Linc, I'll be right behind you."

He led the way outside, gulping in fresh air that was heavy with humidity and moisture. A badly needed rainstorm had blown through, the rain soaking the forest around them. He hoped the soaked exterior of the cabin, along with the wet trees and brush, would prevent the fire from spreading. Scanning the area, he hustled the three women toward his rental. Caitlyn and Annette climbed into the back; Jayme took the front passenger seat.

Without hesitation, he slid behind the wheel, gunned the engine, and drove away from the burning cabin. He heard Jayme calling 911, explaining what had happened, and providing the address to the cabin. She sounded amazingly calm, and he was impressed with her ability to function well in a crisis.

"I don't understand," Caitlyn said in a husky voice. "How did the fire start?"

Linc glanced at Jayme, who turned her head to meet his gaze. He didn't want to frighten the girls more than they were already, yet at the same time, they both needed to understand the seriousness of the situation.

"Someone threw a firebomb through the window," Linc finally said. "I happened to be coming out of the bathroom when it happened." He didn't add that he had a pillow and blanket on the sofa that may have looked as if he was sleeping there.

He didn't doubt for one minute that the arsonist intended to kill him. If for no other reason than to get to Jayme.

Linc's chest was tight as he navigated the dark country road. He couldn't, wouldn't allow that to happen.

"But why did someone throw a firebomb?" Caitlyn persisted.

"Because of me," Jayme said, turning in her seat to look back at her sister. "I told you someone torched my car, threw a firebomb into the physical therapy clinic, and then blew up Linc's car."

There was a long moment of silence as Caitlyn digested this information. Linc wondered if the girl hadn't really believed that her sister had been targeted on purpose.

Glancing in his rearview mirror at Caitlyn's stricken features, he knew she understood the truth now.

"H-how did he find us at the cabin?" Caitlyn asked.

Linc focused on driving and making sure no one was following behind them. He felt Jayme's gaze and shrugged as if to say it was up to her to decide how much to tell the girls.

"It's my fault, isn't it?" Caitlyn said, answering her own question. "Because I went back to the apartment to get our things."

"Don't worry, we're safe now," Jayme said in a soothing tone. "We need to be thankful no one was hurt."

God had been working overtime, watching over them, Linc thought. And he sent up a silent prayer of thanks.

"But if I had come straight to the cabin the way you told me to," Caitlyn began.

"Don't, Cait. We can't go back and fix what happened." Jayme glanced at her sister. "And honestly, we don't know for sure how we were found."

"Jayme is right. I didn't notice anyone following us from Caitlyn's apartment," Linc agreed. "So if we were followed, that's on me." A thought occurred to him. "Maybe the Honda was tracked."

"You mean with a GPS device of some sort?" Jayme asked with a grimace. "At this point, I think it's safe to say anything is possible."

Another precaution I should have taken, Linc thought

grimly. Although honestly, it hadn't occurred to him until after their so-called safe house had been compromised. Maybe he should have considered the possibility, but his experience was in fighting and investigating fires, not general police work.

Captain Barstow needed to be more involved in this thing. Before the next attempt.

"W-where are we going?" Annette asked. The girl had been quiet throughout the ordeal, maybe out of guilt for encouraging Caitlyn to return to their apartment.

As Jayme said, it was too late to go back and change the past. But he wasn't sure how to handle getting the girls to class.

If he had his way, he'd make them skip out. Surely missing one class wouldn't be the end of the world.

"Linc?" Jayme's voice pulled him from his troubled thoughts. "What's your plan on where we should spend the rest of the night?"

"We'll go back to the hotel." It was really the only option. He couldn't find another rental at midnight.

"Not the Shady Lane," Caitlyn complained. "It's so gross."

"No, a much nicer place than that." He caught Caitlyn's gaze in the rearview mirror. "Trust me, okay?"

"Okay." Caitlyn offered a tremulous smile. "And I'm really sorry about taking that detour to our apartment."

"Me too," Annette added earnestly. "I mean, who would have thought we'd be tracked to the cabin? It's like something out of a James Bond movie."

"Worse than a James Bond movie," Caitlyn said in a low tone. "I should have listened to Jayme."

"Next time, right?" Jayme said lightly.

Linc took a long convoluted way to the hotel. He didn't think his SUV was compromised, but the mere possibility required taking extra precautions. At least with a larger hotel their room wouldn't be easy to target.

Especially if he insisted on being on one of the top floors.

He parked near the lobby and quickly whisked everyone inside. They hadn't brought much with them, just phones and power cords, which had been the only easy items to grab. Fifteen minutes later, Linc had safely gotten the three women settled in a large two-bedroom suite.

"This is so nice," Caitlyn gushed, much the same way Jayme had the previous night. That they were so easily impressed only made him feel worse about the situation that was quickly spiraling out of control.

"I'm not tired," Annette complained. "Can we watch a movie?"

Linc had been about to agree, but Jayme cut him off. "No, we're not paying for a movie. This isn't a vacation, we're here to be safe. Both of you need to get some sleep."

"Okay, okay." Cailyn waved her hand. "No need to get crabby."

"I'm heading down to move the car," Linc told Jayme. "Don't open the door to anyone while I'm gone."

"I won't."

He hurried back down to the lobby and took another few moments to examine the undercarriage of his rental. No tracking device had been placed on the vehicle, which made him feel slightly better. He moved the car, parking it well out of sight from the road, then returned to the suite.

As he walked into the room, his phone rang. Recognizing the Sevierville Police Department, he answered, "This is Quade."

"Another fire?" Captain Barstow demanded. "My night

shift sergeant woke me up to let me know it was the location you'd taken Ms. Weston."

"Yes, unfortunately, our location was compromised." Linc sighed and rubbed the back of his neck. The two girls had disappeared into their room, but Jayme was seated on a chair, listening in. "We're all safe, though. We did our best to minimize the fire damage before getting out of there."

"The fire department mentioned that most of the fire had been extinguished by the time they'd arrived," Barstow agreed. "Between the recent rainstorms and the mitigation tactics you deployed, the damage was limited to the main living space. But, Linc, how on earth did this happen?"

It was a valid question. "I need you to send a couple of squads to check out the gray Honda we left in the driveway," Linc directed grimly. "Look for a tracking device. It's the only way I can explain how we were discovered so quickly. Oh, and I checked my rental but didn't find anything."

The captain muttered something harsh under his breath. "Okay, we'll search for the GPS device. I'll be in touch when I hear back from the officers."

"Thanks."

"Where are you now?" Barstow asked.

"A hotel." He wasn't about to give anything more than that. "Call me back when you have information for me."

"Will do." Barstow disconnected from the call.

He dropped onto the sofa, staring glumly around the suite. Apparently, the cabin hadn't been his best idea.

"You really think Caitlyn's car has a tracker on it?" Jayme's serious question drew his gaze. "I mean, who would know enough how to do that?"

"It's not difficult, they're easy to buy and tuck up underneath a bumper." He shook his head. "I should have considered that possibility. Should have insisted they ride with me rather than taking their own car."

"Please don't take responsibility for this," Jayme protested. "Caitlyn owns a piece, and so does Annette. And really, you're the one who keeps telling me that the fault lies with the arsonist. We're the victims of his twisted mind game."

"True." He smiled at how she'd thrown his own words back at him. "As you said, we have a lot to be grateful for. That entire situation could have ended very differently."

"I know." Jayme shifted over so that she could reach out and take his hand. "If you'd been sleeping on the couch . . ."

"Yeah." He gently cupped her hand between his. "I thought of that too. But what worries me the most is that we still don't know who this guy is. I can't find him if I don't know who I'm looking for."

"I have faith in you, Linc. You'll find him."

He was humbled by her statement. "I pray I can do that before anyone gets hurt." He paused, then added, "Especially you."

"I don't want you hurt either. And I even prayed that God would spare us," Jayme admitted softly. "I think you might be right about Him watching over us."

"Really?" He smiled, fiercely glad she'd been able to open her mind and her heart to God. A monumental occasion considering the horror of what she'd lived through. "Oh, Jayme, I'm so happy to hear you say that. Please know God will always be there for you whenever you need Him."

"Well, I'm not an expert at praying or anything," she protested. "But I have to admit, the idea of God protecting and guiding us has given me some comfort." She shrugged, then added, "You were right about the Preacher's lies. I guess I should have realized the man was mentally unhinged. Instead of turning my back on religion, I should have considered seeking the truth."

"You are an incredible woman," he murmured. His gaze locked on hers, awareness sizzling between them. He wasn't entirely sure how it happened, but as he tugged her closer, Jayme wrapped her arms around him. He half expected her to resist, but she eagerly embraced him, burying her face against his chest. She lifted her head and looked deep into his eyes as she kissed him.

Their kiss seemed to go on forever yet was over far too soon. He didn't push, never wanting to take advantage of the forced togetherness, so he cradled her close and reassured her that he'd keep her safe.

Stroking his hand over her silky red hair, he knew in that moment how incredibly difficult it would be to let her go.

———

LINC'S KISS WAS AMAZING, yet so was being held in his arms, almost as if he cherished her. Logically, she knew he still loved his wife and mourned his daughter, but still, his kindness was something rare and precious.

Something she didn't want to let go.

But, of course, they couldn't stay entwined on the sofa forever. His grip loosened, and she forced herself to push away. Instantly, she missed his warmth.

"I—uh, wanted to thank you for saving our lives." She hoped the light was dim enough that he wouldn't notice her blush. Drat her pale skin anyway. "Try to get some rest. I'm sure we'll have another long day tomorrow."

"Yes." His voice was low and gravelly, which only made him sound more attractive. She told herself to get a grip.

The man was being sweet and kind, no reason to make this into some sort of prelude to a relationship.

She was the one who'd kissed him. For the second time.

Not the other way around.

Jayme rose and managed to make her way into the bedroom. Linc had been generous in obtaining a suite, and she hated knowing how much money he'd been forced to spend on her. Would have to keep spending since they had to keep moving from place to place.

And Linc was still no closer to catching this guy.

She tossed and turned, eventually falling into a restless sleep.

It's time for you to make me happy . . .

No! Jayme fought against his grasping hands, the weight of his body pinning her to the sofa, his hot, fetid breath on her face. She reached back, grabbed the lantern, and slammed it into him . . .

Her eyes shot open as the pain of the oil burning her hand jarred her awake. Only the pain wasn't real, not anymore.

Still, she instinctively massaged the scars, taking deep shuddering breaths to calm her racing heart. It was at times like these that she desperately wished there was a way to keep the memories of the past back where they belonged.

Pushing the covers off, she stumbled toward the bathroom, splashing cold water on her face. The temperature in the room was quite comfortable, but reliving those moments of the fire always made her hot and sweaty.

If she were home alone, she'd go into the kitchen to make a cup of tea. But she wasn't home, and Linc was getting some badly needed sleep in the living area.

She sat up against the headboard and raked her fingers through her hair. Was it the fire on the sofa in the cabin that had brought the nightmare back? Understandable at some level, she supposed.

What she needed was a distraction. It never occurred to her to turn on the television set, she didn't have a TV at home and had no interest in flipping through channels to find something to watch.

She'd had to leave her notebook back at the cabin. *Probably gone forever*, she thought with a sigh.

There was a small pad of paper and nubby pencil next to the phone, but she decided against trying to use that. In these situations, she tended to write page after page after page of notes.

Not really focusing on the issues in the past or the future she yearned for. Over the years, she'd made up stories to keep Caitlyn entertained.

Stories she'd recently begun to put on paper. Lately, she'd begun writing adult stories rather than middle grade books. Early in their runaway days, she'd spun tales as a way to distract Caitlyn from the terrible places they'd been forced to live in.

Like the Shady Lane Motel.

Jayme rested her head on her knees and thought about the most recent story she'd started working on. Focusing on the characters and the adventure helped push the memory of the fire aside.

Too bad she'd have to start over with the story she'd been working on at Linc's house. A new idea, one that had some potential.

Or so she hoped. Although from what little she knew about the publishing world, breaking in was nearly impossible to do without obtaining a literary agent.

But that didn't mean she couldn't write the stories. For herself now that Caitlyn was grown up and had moved on.

Maybe one day she'd be able to see her stories in print. Books had been her salvation during the early years of her foster care. When she'd been sent to live with the Preacher, she'd missed having books to read more than anything.

In the back of her mind, she'd thought her stories might provide a sense of hope to other kids stuck in the foster system. Kids who had experiences similar to or even worse than what she and Caitlyn had suffered.

Silly dream, maybe. But just thinking about her story helped push the remnants of the dream away.

Jayme managed to get another two hours of sleep before the rays of sunlight streaming through the window woke her. She padded over to look outside, relieved to notice the dark storm clouds from the night before had vanished, leaving a clear blue sky and plenty of sunshine in its wake.

After washing up in the bathroom, she opened the door to see if Linc was still sleeping. If anyone deserved a couple of extra hours of sleep, it was him.

"Hey." He yawned and scrubbed his jaw as if he'd just woken up. "Thought I heard the shower going."

"Sorry I woke you." She crossed over to where the small coffeemaker was located. "The bathroom is all yours."

"Thanks." He flashed a grin before disappearing into her room.

No surprise the girls were still sleeping. Jayme figured they had stayed up to watch TV, regardless of being denied the chance to pay for a movie. As she watched the coffee drip, she reminded herself that she'd worked hard to provide Caitlyn the best childhood possible. Oh, they'd struggled, lived in terrible places, had often gone hungry, but at the end of the day, she'd kept her sister safe. Supported Caitlyn's going to school so that she'd interact with others and form friendships.

And look where Caitlyn was now, living in her own apartment with Annette and nearly finished with her veterinary tech program.

It had been a long, hard journey to get here, but it was well worth it.

With a surge of renewed determination, she straightened her shoulders. No way was she going to allow this jerk of an arsonist to ruin things now.

She poured a cup of coffee and curled up in the corner of the sofa. There had to be something she was missing. Some connection she was oblivious to.

As always, her mind came back to the Preacher.

Had he survived the fire? Thirteen years was a long time to wait before seeking revenge. And what about the obituary Linc had found? If Simon had escaped, he'd need to have received medical care.

These weren't new considerations, she'd expressed them to Linc two days ago, but maybe she was looking at this wrong.

What if the Preacher had escaped but was burned beyond recognition? If no one had been able to identify him, he could have ended up as a John Doe somewhere. Could right now be walking around Sevierville under a different name.

But even so, she felt certain she'd recognize him. Especially since she knew he'd been burned.

She thought back to the man she'd chased across Sampson's parking lot. When he'd looked at her, she hadn't noticed any obvious scarring to his face. Granted, she'd only gotten a brief glimpse of the man, but a scar would have stood out in her memory. No way was he the Preacher.

Linc emerged from her room looking handsome as ever.

She mentally rolled her eyes at her own foolishness. They didn't have time for this nonsense.

"Hey, thanks for the coffee." Linc made a beeline for the pot. "Are you hungry? We could order breakfast."

She inwardly winced at the cost of ordering room service. "No, I'm fine. We can grab something quick and cheap on the road."

Linc sipped his coffee, but the wary expression in her dark eyes set off alarm bells.

"You told me I could go with you to visit Kevin Leib," she reminded him. "The girls need to go to class anyway."

"I was thinking they'd be better off playing hooky." He lowered his cup and moved over to sit beside her. "Jayme, this firebug put a GPS tracker on your sister's car."

"Captain Barstow confirmed that?"

"Yeah. I had the Honda towed to the garage so we can try lifting fingerprints off the rear bumper, where the device was found."

"That sounds promising." She felt a buzz of excitement at the thought of nailing this guy. "And once we talk to Kevin, we may know more."

"Jayme, you should stay here with the girls. Let me talk to Kevin."

"Please don't make me sit here all day with nothing to do." She held his gaze. "The girls will be fine with a movie, but yesterday dragged by so slowly I could barely stand it. I'm not used to sitting around doing nothing."

He sighed heavily. "Jayme, I can't stand knowing you're in danger. I told you before, I need you to be safe."

"I'll be safe with you." She offered a wan smile. "Devon is a nice guy, but he's so young . . ."

"Devon?" Jayme tried not to groan at the interest in

Caitlyn's voice. She turned to see her sister combing her long blonde hair. "He's coming back to watch over us?"

"Yes," Linc confirmed. "He'll be here soon. I called to let him know about the firebomb at the cabin and our new location. He sounded upset to hear about what happened but is grateful everyone is okay."

"Cool," Caitlyn said. "But what about our class?"

"You'll have to skip it," Jayme told her. "Shouldn't be a problem after you skipped out of work this past weekend."

Her sister winced. "Look, it was one time. One fun concert. It's not like Annette and I make a habit of blowing off work. And I can't skip today, it's our hardest class, lecture in the morning and lab in the afternoon."

Jayme could feel the beginning of a headache pulsing in her temple. "One class isn't going to impact your ability to graduate."

Caitlyn scowled. "But I like my classes."

"The last time you didn't listen to me a fire broke out in the cabin," Jayme reminded her.

"I know, but couldn't Devon take us to school, sit with us, and drive us back here? I don't think that's putting us at an unnecessary risk."

"Linc? I'll leave this one up to you." Jayme wasn't sure what the right answer was anymore. She just wanted this guy caught, and soon.

Linc's phone rang, and he stood and moved toward her bedroom for privacy. Jayme strained to listen but couldn't hear much.

He was back in less than a minute. "No need to head to Nashville," he said.

Her stomach clenched. "Why not?"

"Just heard from Kevin Leib's parole officer, he reached out to save us a trip. Turns out Kevin was in jail all weekend after starting a fire in an old warehouse in Nashville." Linc stared at her. "He's an arsonist, but not our perp."

Jayme closed her eyes and rubbed her temple. It was good to have one name taken off the suspect list, but it wasn't like there were dozens of others.

They'd reached another dead end.

CHAPTER ELEVEN

Linc swallowed a wave of frustration. He'd really hoped Kevin Leib was their guy. An arsonist for hire had made the most sense since the pattern didn't fit the typical firebug. Finding and arresting the arsonist would lead him to the person who'd ultimately decided to target Jayme.

The way these attacks were escalating, he needed something to go on. And soon.

"Now what?" Jayme asked, looking dejected.

"I don't know." He hated feeling so helpless. He stared at his phone. "I'll check with the Memphis parole office. They never got back to me on our other suspect, Terrance Foley."

"Um, I hate to interrupt," Caitlyn said. "But Annette and I really want to attend our classes today. Skipping lab means we'd have to take some sort of make-up session or we won't graduate. Besides, we only have the two classes, the lecture at ten and the lab that starts at one. We'll be finished by three."

He glanced at Jayme who shrugged. "I'm not sure what to do. I don't want them to be in danger, but this is their last semester before graduating. Do you think Devon can keep them safe while they attend?"

"Probably." While the firebug had tracked them to the cabin using a GPS device on Caitlyn's car, he believed Jayme was the main target. Meeting Jayme's intense blue gaze, he sensed she realized that too.

"Thank you, Linc!" Caitlyn flashed a smile. "You're the best." She turned toward her friend. "You want to shower first?"

"Okay." Annette turned and disappeared into the bedroom.

He called Terrance Foley's parole officer in Memphis, but again, no one picked up on the other line. "This is Arson Investigator Lincoln Quade, I really need to talk to you about Foley as soon as possible." He rattled off his phone number, then disconnected the call.

"Over six hours to drive to Memphis," Jayme said grimly. "Would be nice to know the guy was there before making the trip."

"Exactly, I'm not taking the trip until I talk to this guy. For all we know, he's been in jail too." A thought struck him. "You'll need to stick with me while the girls are in class."

Jayme held up her phone. "I've been texting with Sandra, one of the physical therapists from the clinic. Apparently, they want staff to come in and help clean the place up. They're paying us while we're off, so it seems a reasonable request. Once the girls leave for class, you can drop me off if you need to do more work. I'll be surrounded by people."

He hesitated, trying to decide what to do. His plan had been to interview Leib, then review the debris from the cabin fire. The scene will likely be hot, but he could still take a look around. Having Jayme at the clinic for a few hours gave him the time he'd need to do that.

"Okay, that sounds good," he finally agreed. "But you need to make sure you stay near the others. No going off alone."

"I won't," Jayme promised.

A knock at the door had him crossing over to look through the peephole. Devon stood there, again dressed casually. He heard the bedroom door shut and glanced back to see that Caitlyn had disappeared inside the bedroom she shared with Annette, probably because she was dressed in her sleepwear. He opened the door and drew the young officer inside. "Thanks for coming."

"I heard about the Molotov cocktail," Devon said with a frown. "I can't believe that guy tried to burn the place down."

"Actually, I'm not convinced that was his intent." Linc sank into one of the chairs. "Why toss just one of them? And why into the living room onto the sofa?"

"To take you out of the equation," Jayme said quietly. "If you were hurt, the arsonist could have come in and grabbed me."

"We need to catch this guy before he does anything worse." Devon looked far more serious today, which was reassuring.

"I'm trying." His tone sounded testy, so he tried to soften it. "Unfortunately, I'm running out of suspects and haven't uncovered any new leads."

"You'll find him, Linc." Jayme reached over to rest her hand on his arm. "I have faith in you."

"Is there something I can do to help?" Devon asked.

"You can keep Caitlyn and Annette safe while they attend classes today," Linc said.

"What about Jay—Ms. Weston?" Devon glanced over at her.

"I'm heading over to help clean up the PT clinic." Jayme's smile didn't quite reach her eyes. "Since the fire was aimed at me, it's the least I can do."

"I'll drop Jayme off at the clinic, you stick with the girls." Linc waved a hand at the suite. "The plan is that we'll all return here late afternoon."

Devon slowly nodded. "You're the boss."

Linc wondered if Devon thought he was off his rocker for allowing Jayme to go to the PT clinic. He pulled out his phone and stared at the screen. Nothing from Terrance Foley's parole officer.

He hoped and prayed there would be some clue outside the cabin fire. Something he could use to track this firebug.

It nagged at him that this guy hadn't made a single mistake.

Linc wanted to believe that he would because no one was perfect. Considering the way the attacks were escalating, this guy was bound to slip up. To leave something behind.

But that needed to happen sooner rather than later.

They sat in silence for a few minutes. "I'll check on the girls." Jayme rose and crossed over to their room.

"You really don't have any solid leads?" Devon asked quietly. "Ms. Weston must have given you an idea of who might want to harm her."

"There are two possibilities, but neither have panned out so far." Linc filled Devon in on the Preacher and Marco Edgar. He glossed over Jayme's and Caitlyn's experiences with the Preacher, but he could see the story disturbed the young cop.

"Just when you think you've heard it all," Devon muttered.

"Yeah." Linc rubbed the back of his neck. "The GPS tracking device concerns me. We need to be extra vigilant about checking to make sure our vehicles are clean."

"I should have thought of that possibility," Devon admitted.

"Me too." Linc couldn't quite shake off the guilt that he'd missed it. "But at least we know what to look for. I need you to be on high alert while the girls are in class. Report in if you see anyone with a scar or who generally looks out of place. I can't imagine our arsonist will blend in well with the college crowd."

"I will." Devon's expression was serious and determined. "No one will hurt them on my watch."

Linc glanced over his shoulder, the women were still inside the bedroom. "And that means no flirting. I know the girls are very pretty, but you can't afford to be distracted."

Devon winced, then nodded. "I understand."

"Good." Linc clapped him on the shoulder. "I'm counting on you."

"Linc, I don't need you to pay me for my time today."

He lifted a brow. "Why not? That was our deal. I pay you to protect the women while I'm unable to be there."

"I know, but they're in danger, and it doesn't feel right to take your money." Devon leveled him a look. "This is what cops do. We protect those in danger."

"Yes, but we don't usually work for free," Linc felt compelled to point out.

"It's still part of the job," Devon insisted. "I don't want your money."

His opinion of the young cop went up several notches. Maybe yesterday Devon had taken the job thinking it wouldn't be a big deal, but today, he had his head screwed on straight. "We'll argue about payment later."

Devon looked exasperated but didn't say anything more as Jayme emerged from the bedroom.

"They'll be out soon. You'll need to stop for breakfast along the way." A hint of a smile flashed over her features. "They're both starving."

If anyone knew what it was really like to go without eating, it was Jayme. He wondered how many meals she'd skipped in order to make sure Caitlyn had something to eat. Probably more than he wanted to know.

He admired Jayme so much. What she'd accomplished despite all the strikes against her. The way she'd cared for her sister over the past thirteen years.

He couldn't bear the thought of the arsonist getting to her.

"I'd be happy to take them through a fast-food drive-through for breakfast," Devon said. "It's not a problem."

"Thanks." Jayme reached for her purse, but Linc held up his hand.

"I'll take care of it. It's part of our protection detail," he added.

"We can settle up later." Devon stuck his hands in his pockets, clearly determined to be an equal partner in this.

"Sorry to keep you waiting," Caitlyn said. She and Annette had both showered, but they were still wearing the same clothes as yesterday.

They all were, except for Devon.

"Not a problem. Are you both ready to go?" Devon asked politely.

Caitlyn glanced at Jayme for a brief moment. "Are you sure you're okay with this plan?"

"Fine. But you stay with Devon at all times and come

straight back here after class," Jayme said firmly. "No arguments."

"Got it." Caitlyn turned toward Devon. "We're ready."

"Take the back exit," Linc said. "Do your best to stay out of sight."

The girls looked at each other, then nodded.

"I've got our exit strategy planned out," Devon assured him. "And I'll be vigilant about the car too. Don't worry, I've got this under control."

"Good." Linc forced a smile. "Be safe."

A minute later, he and Jayme were alone in the suite.

"I hope I didn't make a mistake letting them go to class," Jayme murmured. "I'll never forgive myself if something happens to them."

"I don't think they're the target, Jayme. And Devon will watch over them. We had a good talk, and he's well aware of the danger and the precautions he needs to take. He's a cop, I know he'll protect them with his life if necessary."

Jayme paled. "I hope it doesn't come to that."

"Me too." Linc glanced at his watch. "We should head out soon. I'm sure you'd like to grab a bite to eat."

"Okay." Jayme looked around the room, then checked for her room key. "Let's go."

He led the way down the hall to a back stairwell. "I know we're on the sixth floor, but down is relatively easy, right?"

This time she smiled for real. "Right."

When they reached the lobby, he took her through another rear door that was labeled as the employee exit. Ignoring the sign, he opened the door and glanced around the rear parking lot. Seeing nothing out of place, he turned toward Jayme. "Stay here, I'm going to check the SUV again for a GPS device."

"Okay."

He strode toward the car and went down on his haunches, checking beneath the entire undercarriage of the car. He took his time and thankfully didn't find anything. He returned to the doorway where he'd left Jayme. "All clear. Let's go."

"This is the same route Devon took the girls?" Jayme asked as they hurried over to the vehicle.

"Yes." He opened her door, then ran around to the driver's side. "Why?"

Her smile widened. "Just thinking about how much they'll complain when the time comes to head back up to the sixth floor."

He chuckled. "But not you." He started the car and drove around the building. "You'd never complain about something as mundane as going up six flights of steps."

"It's nothing compared to walking through the mountains," she agreed. "Although I'm definitely out of shape now."

"You're not." Thinking of how great she'd felt in his arms had him changing the subject. "What would you like for breakfast?"

She waved a hand. "Anything that has a breakfast sandwich is fine."

Linc made sure to take a circuitous route away from the hotel, checking often to make sure they weren't followed. When he was satisfied, he pulled into the first fast-food joint they came across.

After getting their food, he backed into a parking spot so the rear bumper was up against a nearby building.

Jayme opened the bag of food and handed him one of the sandwiches. Then she took hers but didn't unwrap it. Instead, she surprised him by reaching for his hand.

Humbled, he gently squeezed her fingers, bowed his head, and prayed. "Dear Lord, we are so very grateful for Your guidance and protection. Please continue to show us the way to safety. Amen."

"Amen," Jayme whispered.

"Thanks for joining me in prayer." He reluctantly released her hand so he could unwrap his sandwich. "You're an inspiration, Jayme."

"What?" Her eyebrows rose in surprise. "Why? I only did what was necessary to survive."

"Yes, but under extremely difficult circumstances. I lost my family to a fire when I was twelve, but my aunt Becca swooped in to take care of me. I know you did the same thing for Caitlyn."

"You've suffered a lot of loss, Linc." Her gaze was intense. "I'm not sure how you managed to survive that."

"None of it was easy," he agreed. "We're both survivors, Jayme. And God will always be our strength."

She nodded but didn't say anything more. He knew the idea of God and faith was very new to her. Yet he was proud at how far she'd come in the few short days they'd been together.

When they'd finished eating, he went through the drive-through again for coffee, then hit the road. The physical therapy clinic wasn't far, and when he pulled up, he was glad to see several other clinic employees were already at the site as well.

"Thanks for the ride." Jayme glanced at him as she opened the car door. "I'll text you when we're finished."

"Okay, but if I don't hear from you by three o'clock, I'll come pick you up. I think it would be a good idea if we meet the girls at the hotel."

"That works, although I doubt we'll be here that long."

Jayme slid out from the car, holding her coffee in one hand. "See you later."

"Bye." He waited and watched as she crossed over to join her colleagues. They all went inside the clinic, but he couldn't see much because the large broken window had already been boarded up.

Linc shook off a sense of unease as he put the SUV into gear and drove off. Jayme wasn't alone. No need for him to be concerned.

Yet, as he turned to head back through town toward the rented cabin, he sent up a silent prayer for her safety.

———

JAYME THREW herself into the physical labor of cleaning up the mess left behind by the firebomb. The water damage was by far worse than what had been done by the fire itself. When she went into the lobby area, she was surprised to see that much like the incident at the cabin, the fire had been localized to the spot where the firebomb had landed.

Several of the plastic lobby chairs had melted into a pile of goo. They reeked of smoke, too, as she and Sandra hauled them out to the large dumpster out back.

"I'm telling you, girl, it's a good thing the clinic was closed when this happened," Sandra said with a frown. "Can you imagine what would have happened to anyone sitting in the lobby when that thing came flying through the window?"

The scene of the cabin fire was still fresh in her mind. "Yes, we should be very grateful no one was hurt."

"Don't know what this world is coming to," Sandra groused. "Seems people just don't know how to behave anymore."

Jayme swallowed hard and nodded. She couldn't shake the guilt that destroying the clinic had been done to lash out at her.

Not that Linc had proof of that theory. Other than the fact that she was a common denominator in each of the recent incidents.

She did her best to push those thoughts aside. One of the physical therapists, a guy named Jake Randal, was huddled with their equipment maintenance guy as they examined the various workout machines. Those that didn't have motors seemed to be working fine, like the free weights and the resistance weights. But the elliptical machine, the stationary bike, and the treadmill were all waterlogged.

"These all need to be replaced." The maintenance guy sighed. "Seems like such a waste, though, as the equipment is barely five years old."

"Yeah." Jake gestured to them. "Let's haul them outside to the dumpster."

The two men wrestled the heavy equipment past her. It made Jayme's heart ache to know how much damage had been caused by this creep. Part of the walls, the equipment, and the lobby furniture, in addition to the large window, would all have to be replaced. Hardly any of what they'd found so far was salvageable.

And for what? Just to scare her?

No. She shivered. There was no denying the ultimate goal was to kill her.

Marco Edgar? Or was it possible the Preacher really was alive and somehow setting these fires?

"Jayme? Can you start going through these supplies?" Sandra asked.

She dragged her gaze from the gym. "Sure."

"Anything that's water damaged needs to be tossed."

Sandra pulled a garbage can over. "But if the packaging is intact and not wet or showing signs of being water damaged, then we can keep it."

"Got it." Jayme began going through the supplies. In the background, she could hear the sound of a buzz saw as damp and/or water-damaged drywall was being removed from the lobby walls. Apparently, it was necessary to do this in order to prevent mold from growing.

Jayme was learning more about fire and water damage than she'd ever wanted to know.

They worked until noon. Jake had ordered sub sand-wiches for them, and they sat outside on the grassy portion in front of the building to eat. Jayme took a quick moment to silently thank God for the food, not bold enough to actu-ally pray in front of anyone else, before digging into her meal.

Overhead, puffy white clouds dotted the sky, yet despite the sun's brightness, the air was cool. The leaves on the trees were a vibrant red, orange, and yellow today, the peak of autumn. For a moment, she thought about how far she'd come from the night of the attempted assault by the Preacher. How she and Caitlyn had grown and thrived over the years.

It made her yearn to know about the other foster kids. Something she should have thought about before now.

Maybe once this arsonist had been found and arrested, she could ask Linc for help in trying to find the rest of her foster siblings. To offer her home to any of them who might need it. To her shame, she didn't know any of their last names. The Preacher's cabin wasn't that kind of environ-ment. The seven of them had only been alone at night, down in the cellar, and most of their discussions had been around escaping the horror of the Preacher. Or on what they'd do once they'd gotten away.

Looking back, she realized they'd probably spent too much time talking about what their lives would be like once they'd escaped from the Preacher's cabin rather than getting to know each other. A silly mistake when they should have been focused on creating an escape plan.

The attempted assault and the fire had not been planned. But it had ultimately worked to their advantage.

God's hand helping them to escape? Maybe. But if that were the case, why had they been forced to live with him for so many years? Well, all except for Caitlyn who'd only been with them for two.

She didn't have a good answer for the questions swirling through her mind. And maybe it didn't matter anymore. Linc would tell her that all of this, even the arsonist stalking her now, was part of God's master plan.

A plan she didn't understand.

"You okay, Jayme?" Sandra asked.

"Fine." She forced a smile. "Feeling a little over-whelmed at the amount of damage. Any idea when they'll reopen?"

"Not yet." Sandra sighed. "It's a matter of getting the drywall repaired and the replacement equipment brought in."

Jayme's heart sank. "Sounds like that could take weeks."

"At least one week, maybe two," Sandra agreed.

Jayme told herself not to panic about paying her mort-gage. Thankfully, October had been paid, so it was a matter of saving money for next month's loan installment. "I may have to get a part-time job as a waitress in the meantime."

"Don't get another job just yet," Sandra protested. "The

owners are working with the insurance company to pay our salaries while the repairs are being completed."

Jayme nodded, but she didn't trust that would happen. And even if it did, there was no guarantee she'd see the money deposited in her bank account by the time the mortgage was due. A job would help tide her over, just in case.

She made a mental note to ask Linc to stop at some of the local restaurants so she could apply for a job. She wasn't above washing dishes, she'd done it before.

"Ready to head back inside?" Jake asked as he came around with a paper bag to collect their garbage. "We should be able finish up soon."

"Ready." She dropped her balled-up sandwich paper into the bag and rose to her feet. Inside, she went back to sorting through what was left of the supplies.

"Hey, we can save some of these for mission trips," Jake said when he came over to see what she was doing.

"Mission trips?" She looked up at him. "What do you mean?"

"There are a couple of surgeons and nurses at the hospital who go on mission trips to third world countries to care for patients who don't have access to modern medicine." He gestured to the bag of wet supplies. "They would take those in a heartbeat."

"But—the sterility is broken," she protested.

"Yeah, I know. But those countries don't have sterile instruments or supplies now." He picked up a water-stained package of gauze. "The docs and nurses would rather use this on their patients' wounds instead of used clothing."

"Wow." Jayme was shocked, but as someone who'd eaten food from the garbage, she totally understood. "Okay, I'll make another pile of supplies that can be donated."

"Great, thanks." He flashed an encouraging smile, then moved on.

Jayme went through the entire stock of supplies for a second time until she had three piles. One labeled for the mission trip, one that could be kept for clinic use. The third and, unfortunately, the largest of the three piles still needed to be taken to the dumpster.

Seemed a waste, but nothing she could do about it.

Jayme lugged the large plastic bag of supplies outside the back door. Using all of her muscles, she struggled to lift it up and over the edge of the dumpster.

"Miss Jayme? Let me help you with that."

She turned to see Mr. Shepard shuffling toward her. "Oh, no, really, I've got it." The poor man didn't look strong enough to lift a library book, much less a bag of damaged supplies.

Still, he did his best using a hand to help push the bag over the rim. "Thanks," she said breathlessly. Then she frowned. "What are you doing here?"

"I came for my regular appointment." Mr. Shepard looked distressed. "I didn't know the clinic had been damaged."

"Oh, you should have gotten a phone call and an email," she said, feeling bad for the guy. "Sorry about that."

"The fire was a terrible thing, wasn't it?" He surprised her by reaching out to grasp her elbow in a firm grip.

The guy was stronger than he let on, but she managed to smile. "It's terrible, but in a week or two, everything will be back to normal."

As she tried to move toward the door, his grip tightened. Then he used his index finger to make a little circle around her elbow.

A wave of nausea hit hard. Jayme froze as she looked at

the old man. Up close, she could see his one good eye boring into hers.

In that moment, the truth hit with the force of a tsunami.

Mr. Shepard was the Preacher!

CHAPTER TWELVE

Linc stood surveying the damaged interior of the cabin. The fire hadn't spread very far, the bulk of the damage was to the sofa. The pillow he'd tossed on one end was nothing but a charred lump.

Reinforcing how close he'd come to being burned or worse.

Dead.

Swallowing his frustration, he reminded himself to stay focused. This guy had to make a mistake, they always did. He turned and cast his gaze around, searching for clues. The cabin interior looked similar to what had been left of the physical therapy clinic lobby, and he felt certain the exact same firebomb had been constructed for both incidents.

The lingering scent of kerosene only reinforced his thought.

He'd gone to the local camping equipment shops to find out if anyone remembered selling kerosene recently. No one had, all explaining how most of their equipment was sold earlier in the tourist season, not early October when things were winding down. Lots of kerosene had been sold earlier in the year, but none in the past month.

Had the accelerant been purchased by this arsonist a while ago? If so, this was a series of attacks that had been deliberately planned ahead of time.

Linc blew out a breath and headed back outside. The area had been taped off as a crime scene, but he nodded to the officer who let him cross over.

"We have a footprint flagged." One of the officers waved toward it. His nametag identified him as Simons. "Looks to be a size ten shoe, probably male, although no way to know for certain."

Linc crouched down beside the footprint. The sole was that of your typical sneaker, and not a brand he recognized. He looked up. "Do you know what type of shoe?"

"We're running it through the database, but we can already rule out Nike, Adidas, ASICS, and New Balance." Officer Simons shrugged. "We'll know more soon."

"I need that information as soon as possible." Linc stared down at the footprint, wondering if it had been left by a woman or a man? His gut told him the latter, and if so, the guy couldn't be very tall or heavy. The footprint would have sunk deeper into the soil if the guy was carrying around a lot of extra weight.

It was their first real clue, although not one that would immediately lead them to the arsonist. Still, he was encouraged and continued searching the area where the firebug had stood to launch his Molotov cocktail.

But he didn't find anything else. The guy must have shown up, lobbed the bomb through the window, then taken off. Frankly, that's what he'd have done if he were intent on doing someone harm. He frowned, realizing Size Ten must have parked along the road and walked up to the property.

Spinning on his heel, he ducked under the crime scene tape and made his way down the rutted gravel driveway. He went slowly, searching for more footprints, but the gravel drive was not conducive to footprints, and he didn't find anything useful.

Upon reaching the road, he glanced both ways, trying to imagine where Size Ten had parked. He turned to the left, thinking the guy may have gone past the driveway to leave his vehicle in order to ensure the best chance of escaping without being seen. If by some miracle Linc had been able to get down the driveway in time to see anything, a car heading past the driveway would have caught his immediate attention, maybe even enough to get a good look at the make and model.

A vehicle driving away wouldn't have given him anything to go on.

Armed with his theory, Linc searched along the side of the road, stopping abruptly when he found tire tread marks in the soft earth next to the asphalt. Using his phone, he snapped a couple of pictures, feeling good about having another clue they could use to track this guy.

Still, it wasn't enough. Tire tracks and shoe prints would come in handy once they had a suspect in custody. But until then, there were dozens of cars and types of shoes that would send them spinning in circles as they attempted to narrow their pool of suspects.

"Did you find something?"

Linc glanced over to see that Officer Simons, the cop who'd spoken to him about the shoe print, had followed him. "Yes, tire marks possibly left by our perp."

"Hmm." Simons crouched down beside them. "Good eye. We'll get these flagged and put into the database too."

"The sooner you can get me the information, the

better." Linc knew they were doing their best, but an intense sense of urgency wouldn't leave him alone. "I know you're swamped, but this is the fifth attack against Ms. Jayme Weston over the past three days. I'm very concerned the next attempt is only hours away."

"I hear you." Simons stood. "I gotta say, in my five years on the force, I've never had so many fire calls."

"Me either," Linc admitted.

"Really? Even as an arson investigator?" Simons asked.

"Yeah, this is over the top. Which is why I'm concerned about where this guy will choose to strike next."

Simons whistled. "Understood.

"Thanks." Linc turned and trekked back up to the cabin. As he walked up the gravel driveway, he tried to imagine the perp doing this with a firebomb in his hand. There was a slight incline, and if the guy was out of shape, he'd have been breathing heavily by the time he'd reached the cabin.

Not that it had stopped him from tossing the bomb through the window. Although maybe it explained his timing being off.

No way to know for sure. He mentally kicked himself again for not thinking to check for a GPS device on Caitlyn's car. Thankfully, no one had been hurt in this most recent attempt.

He believed God was watching over them, yet he couldn't deny the chances of this guy succeeding in hurting someone, specifically Jayme, was growing by the moment.

His phone buzzed, and he glanced down at the text message from Devon. The young cop had done a one-eighty in his attitude toward his protection assignment. Devon had kept him updated throughout the day.

Lunch break is over. C and A are safe in class.

Thanks. Linc texted back. *Let me know when you leave to return to the hotel.*

Will do.

He stared at the phone for a moment, itching to call Jayme, but forced himself to slip the device back into his pocket. She was fine at the clinic, surrounded by employees. His nagging desire to hear her voice concerned him. He shouldn't be so wrapped up in Jayme's life, caring about her on a personal level.

Gina and Melody were his entire life once. The last thing he wanted to do was experience that level of loss again.

Yet he couldn't seem to get Jayme out of his mind.

Out of his heart.

He gave himself a mental shake and continued working the scene. It was only on his way back to his vehicle that he saw the tiny slip of paper stuck to a pricker bush.

With a frown, he crossed over to look at it more closely.

The fragment was smaller than the size of a dime, yet there was just the slightest tip of a teal-colored triangle visible along the bottom. He frowned, wondering if he was going overboard with his attempt to search for clues. This piece of paper could have been left by anyone.

Then he remembered the storm that had come through earlier in the day. The paper was too small to check for fingerprints, so he tested the edge of it with his index finger, verifying it was indeed dry.

Which meant it must have been left after the rain.

He turned and tracked down Simons. "I found something else," he said.

"Show me."

Linc led the way back to the tiny slip of paper. Simons hunkered down to see it more closely. "I know it doesn't look like much," he explained to the cop. "But it's dry, which makes me think it may have been left by our perp. The firebomb was tossed through the window after the rainstorm blew through."

"It's pretty small." Simons's voice was laced with doubt. "We won't be able to get any usable prints from something this."

"I know. But I think we should keep it as evidence anyway." Linc wasn't sure why the scrap of paper bothered him. It seemed a bit of a stretch to think the perp had left it there on the bush, even by accident.

Unless . . . he frowned. What if there had been something tucked in the guy's pocket? The paper may have snagged on the thorny bush as the guy eased by.

Too bad a larger chunk of the paper hadn't been left behind. Something that would have given him a clue as to who this guy was.

And what grudge he was holding against Jayme.

After taking a picture of the discovery, Simons placed the scrap of paper in an evidence bag. "It's a long shot, but maybe we can track something related to that aqua color on the tip."

"Thanks." Finding three clues was excellent, more than any of the other fire scenes had provided.

But it wasn't enough.

After spending another thirty minutes and not finding anything of significance, Linc left the cabin. Officer Simons promised to stay in touch, and he prayed he'd hear something about the tire track and the shoe print very soon.

His stomach rumbled with hunger. He had his computer, so he stopped at a local diner that offered free Wi-Fi for a quick meal. He took his computer inside to work. He tried to find more arsonists who had been recently released from jail and found one more guy, Waylon James, who'd been released two years ago. His last-known address was Nashville. It was a stretch, but he still made the call to the Nashville PD asking for anything they might have on Waylon. When that was finished, he poked through shoe websites to find one that matched the image on his phone.

To his surprise, he stumbled across a sturdy orthopedic type of shoe. The three circles on the sole were a direct match to the print found outside the cabin.

Was their perp an older guy? Like maybe the Preacher?

He finished eating and called Officer Simons to let him know about the orthopedic shoe he'd found online.

"Good work, Linc. I'll let our captain know."

"Thanks." Linc put his phone away, closed his computer, and left money for his bill before hurrying out of the diner.

Maybe it was crazy, but he couldn't fight the desperate need to head over to the physical therapy clinic. He told himself it would be nice to know how the cleanup process was coming along.

But he knew the real reason was that he had to see Jayme for himself. To see with his own eyes that she was doing okay.

The trip didn't take long, and some of the tension eased from his shoulders when he noticed a man and a woman standing outside the clinic. He slid out of the rental SUV and hurried over. "How is it going?"

"Ah, good. We're just about finished," the man said. "I'm Jake by the way."

"Linc Quade," he introduced himself.

"Oh, Linc. I'm glad you're here." A sweet African American woman turned to face him. "I'm Sandra, and I've heard about you from Jayme." He was ridiculously pleased to hear it. Before he could say anything, though, Sandra went on. "I thought Jayme was with you, but now I'm worried she's missing."

"Missing?" He grasped her arm. "When? How long ago?"

"Just, ah," Sandra glanced helplessly at Jake. "Not that long. Maybe twenty to thirty minutes?"

Jake nodded. "I left her sorting supplies. It looks to me like she finished, there are two piles, one marked keep, the other marked donations."

Linc didn't care about the supplies. "Thirty minutes? And you didn't call anyone?"

"I honestly thought she was with you, Linc." Sandra's expression was full of distress. "She told me you dropped her off and would be back to pick her up. We didn't realize right away that she was gone."

Linc struggled to breathe, to focus. "Could she be in the restroom or something?" He forced the words past his tight throat.

"I looked," Sandra said. "But come inside, see for yourself."

Linc went into the clinic building, barely registering the progress they'd made in cleaning the place out. He did notice the teal-colored logo on the wall and remembered the teal color on the slip of paper.

Was it possible one of their physical therapy patients had targeted Jayme after all?

Jake went over to where there was a chair and stacks of supplies. "This is where Jayme was working."

Linc stared down at the empty spot, his gut tightening with fear. "She couldn't have left out the front, you guys would have noticed, right?"

"Right," Sandra agreed.

"I bet she took a bunch of the damaged, beyond use supplies to the dumpster out back," Jake said, moving through the clinic to the back door.

Linc hoped, prayed they'd find Jayme back there. Maybe she'd fallen and hurt herself, breaking her phone and lying on the ground, waiting for them to come find her.

But no. The area around the dumpster and the rest of the alley was empty.

He stood for a moment, crushed beneath a wave of guilt. He never should have let her come here today. Never!

What if she died because of his failure?

Linc wanted to scream in frustration but forced himself to think. Think! Jayme must have brought the garbage out here. Had the perp staked the place out? Had he waited for her to show up alone before making his move?

His gaze fell on a long skinny piece of plastic. He bent and picked it up. "Is this something that would have fallen out of the bag of damaged supplies?"

"No," Sandra replied without hesitation. "It's the cap of a needle, but everything was in packages, right, Jake? We don't store needles all by themselves. And where is the needle portion? The cap wouldn't have dropped off the needle hub that easily."

"Sandra is right," Jake agreed. He gazed around the area. "I'd say it was left by a drug user." He grimaced. "Which makes me think we should get this dumpster picked up ASAP so other drug users don't crawl in to get the supplies."

"Drug users." Linc stared at the needle cap. "If that were the case, wouldn't there be other signs of drug paraphernalia here? Have you seen this problem before?"

"I've never seen anyone using drugs around here, and you're right, if that were the case, we'd see other things, like syringe wrappers or tourniquets." Sandra frowned. "It's odd to have just the needle cover on the ground."

Linc feared the cap was proof that Jayme had been accosted back here, drugged, and then taken away.

But where?

"I need a patient list ASAP," Linc said in a hoarse voice. "And don't tell me about patient privacy concerns, Jayme's life is at stake here."

Jake and Sandra glanced at each other, then reluctantly nodded.

Linc's relief was short-lived. Going through the patient list would take time. Time Jayme didn't have.

Please, Lord, please keep Jayme safe in Your care! Give me the strength and knowledge to find her before it's too late!

JAYME'S MOUTH felt like cotton, her brain foggy as she slowly regained consciousness. It took her a moment to realize she was sitting in a kitchen chair, her hands tied behind her back, her feet bound together at the ankles.

Every muscle in her body screamed with pain when she tried to move. She lifted her head, horrified to realize she was in her house. In her kitchen, tied to one of her own chairs.

Memories cascaded over her. Memories of the past, living in the cellar of the Preacher's cabin, and the more recent memory where she'd realized Mr. Shepard was the Preacher.

All this time, the Preacher had been alive. Alive!

Her mind had trouble comprehending what had just happened.

Not just that the Preacher was still alive but that he'd managed to find her after all this time. Thirteen years!

And that he was the one who'd been starting the fires, throwing firebombs through the clinic window and last night into the cabin.

Why hadn't she recognized him?

"Well, I see you're finally awake."

Her entire body shuddered with revulsion at his voice. It was different now compared to back then.

Everything about him was different—his looks, his personality, or the one he'd pretended to have.

But not that creepy way he rubbed her elbow.

She wanted to close her eyes, to crawl inside herself, pretend he wasn't there. But she forced herself to straighten her spine, to meet his gaze.

Jayme had managed to escape from him once. She had to believe she could do it again.

Although being tied up like a Thanksgiving turkey would add a layer of difficulty. Where was Mrs. Katz? Would she notice something was wrong and call the police?

She was afraid to bank on it.

"I'm impressed to see you here in Sevierville." Jayme hoped he couldn't hear the slight tremor in her tone. "I really hoped you'd burned to death in the fire."

She mentally braced herself to feel his wrath, but he surprised her by letting out a harsh cackle. "Oh, I'm sure you would have loved that, *Jayme*." The way he said her name made her skin crawl. "But as you can see, I survived."

She thought about what Linc had discovered about the human remains being unable to be identified. "And being the coward that you are, I assume you left your dear wife, Ruth, behind to die?"

Anger flashed in his eyes, making her regret goading

him. "You're the coward, *Jayme*." He waved a hand. "But that doesn't matter any longer. Now that I have you here, you'll get exactly what you deserve."

Her throat was so dry from whatever drug he'd given her she couldn't swallow. She had no idea how long she'd been knocked out, how long she'd been gone from the clinic.

Had Sandra and Jake called Linc to let him know she was gone?

Even if they had, there's no way in the world Linc would think to come to her own house to find her.

Linc. Despite her dehydrated state, tears pricked her eyes. He'd blame himself for this even though she was the one who'd insisted on going to the clinic.

She was the one who hadn't recognized Mr. Shepard as the Preacher until it was too late.

The Preacher pulled a small blue plastic tube from his pocket. When he flicked his thumb over the top, a flame ignited.

A lighter.

Somehow, she instinctively knew that the best way for her to stay alive would be to keep him talking. She had to believe Linc would find her. She twisted her bound hands, trying to loosen the rope.

"I'm impressed you weren't more badly injured from the fire," she said, forcing herself to look directly at his face. "I mean, that long jagged scar on your cheek looks like a knife wound, not a burn."

"You mean this?" He reached up to touch the red jagged scar. Then he dug his fingers into his face, peeling off several layers of rubbery material revealing the burn scars beneath. "I did this for your benefit, *Jayme*." He moved close enough that she wanted to shirk from his evil smile. "I knew you'd be on the lookout for a man with a burn on his face, so I simply changed it to look like something else."

She hadn't given him enough credit. Not just the strength and determination to escape thirteen years ago, but even now. The man was crazy smart like a fox. Completely insane, but crazy smart.

"You fooled me," she admitted, continuing to work at the bindings around her wrists. They were painfully tight, to the point she wasn't sure she'd be able to get free. "I really thought you were a wounded trauma patient."

"That's because you only saw what I wanted you to see." He took another step closer, flicking the lighter in his hand. On and off. On and off. "Do you have any idea how long I spent in the hospital because of you?"

"Oh, you mean because I fought back when you tried to rape me?" She winced as the lighter came closer. "What did you think would happen? If you'd have left me alone, you never would have gotten burned."

The lighter flicked on and off.

It took every ounce of willpower she possessed not to rear back from the flame. To keep her gaze on his disfigured face instead of the lighter.

"I had surgery, after surgery, after surgery." He stared down at her with his good eye. "The pain was crippling, but they didn't let up. Dressing changes, then more surgery." He leaned in. "There isn't enough fire in the world to make up for what you put me through."

Fire.

Her inner strength began to crumble. She'd feared this was his plan. To burn her as badly as he'd been burned.

Fire. The element she hated the most would be how he finally killed her.

Dear Lord, help me! Please, don't let him do this! Save me!

The Preacher flicked the lighter right in front of her eyes, close enough that she could feel the little bit of heat, smell the lighter fluid.

"I know your real name is Simon." She pushed the words through clenched teeth. "Simon Penske."

The lighter flicked off as he reared back in surprise. "How did you know that?"

"Ruth slipped up and used it once. The arson investigator helping me found your obituary." She tried to smile. "That was really clever to pretend you were dead."

"It was," he agreed. His good eye narrowed. "But I have to admit, I didn't realize you and Quade had gotten that far."

"Linc is a very smart man. And he's determined to find you."

The evil smile was back. "Well, he hasn't. And he won't find you, until it's too late."

She could read the intent in his eyes. The Preacher was going to kill her by setting her house on fire.

Maybe setting her on fire first.

She was so afraid she almost threw up what remained of the sub sandwich sitting like lard in her gut. She forced the nausea away and kept talking. "Did you ever find the other foster kids?"

"Why would I bother?" He flicked the lighter on again, staring at the flame as if mesmerized. It occurred to her in that moment that he really was the antithesis of God.

He was the devil. Pure evil, all the way through.

"You're the only one I wanted, *Jayme*." The emphasis on her name was wreaking havoc with her effort to remain emotionally detached. "Once I kill you, my mission will be complete."

"Really? That seems rather pathetic. I mean, I'm flattered that I've been your sole mission for so many years." She had no idea why she was goading him again, the words tumbling out of her so fast she didn't have time to comprehend what she was saying. "You're a powerful man, *Simon*. What good is killing one woman? Don't you have anything else important to do in your life?"

He lashed out at her, his fist slamming into her jaw. Pain reverberated through her, but she would rather have the fist than the fire.

Please, Lord, not the fire!

"Enough!" He spun away and paced back and forth, clearly trying to get himself under control. Jayme strained at the bindings, craning her neck in an effort to see the time on the microwave clock. Four o'clock in the afternoon.

Caitlyn and Annette would be finished with their lab by now. Devon would have driven them to the hotel. She'd purposefully not mentioned Caitlyn by name so as not to put any ideas in the Preacher's warped mind.

Linc would know by now that she'd been taken. He was out there, right this minute, trying to find her.

The Preacher spun around and smiled again. "It's time."

No! Not yet! Please, God, not yet!

He turned and walked over to the door. She belatedly noticed the large can of kerosene he must have brought in while she'd been out.

Fear tumbled over her in full force. If the Preacher doused her with the kerosene, it would only take one flick of his lighter to start her on fire.

CHAPTER THIRTEEN

"Where's my sister?" Caitlyn's concern was etched on her features. Linc understood because he couldn't quell the overwhelming sense of panic either.

"Trust me, I'm going to find her."

"How?" Caitlyn demanded.

It was a fair question. Since leaving the clinic, he'd notified the police about Jayme's abduction and had spoken directly to Captain Barstow about putting out a notice to all officers to keep on the lookout for her. He'd scanned the list of patients Jake and Sandra had provided to him with his phone app and had emailed that to Barstow too.

Then he'd reviewed the list of clinic patients over the past year for himself. Unfortunately, there were more than he'd anticipated. Too many possibilities to narrow them down to a handful of suspects.

He reviewed the list again, looking for anything out of place. The only name that struck him as being odd was Adam K. Shepard.

Not a wildly different name exactly, but the biblical reference had given him pause. Did the K stand for King?

Was it possible this was really Simon Penske, the Preacher? He'd reviewed the list again and couldn't come up with anything else. And he couldn't afford to discount the possibility. The fact that the patient had an apartment near the clinic only added to his concern. He'd used his computer to look up the guy's DMV records, grimacing when he saw an older man with a scar running down his cheek. It didn't look like a burn scar, but the disfigurement convinced him he was on the right track.

He continued digging into the guy's background, praying he wasn't taking the wrong path in following this guy when the real culprit was someone else entirely. According to the DMV, Shepard drove a blue Chevy Spark. The Spark made him feel as if he was indeed on the right track. Armed with the vehicle information and Shepard's address, Linc rose and strode to the hotel door. "Caitlyn, you need to stay here with Devon, okay? I'll let you know as soon as I find her."

Caitlyn nodded while Annette put an arm around her friend. Devon's expression was grim, but he gave Linc a nod. "I'll take care of them."

"Thanks." He believed the young man would. Linc quickly left the hotel, rushing out the back door to his SUV. He wasn't worried about being followed any longer now that the arsonist had what he wanted.

Jayme.

Linc forced himself to stay focused. He'd promised Caitlyn he'd find her.

He'd promised himself too.

Whoever had grabbed Jayme had drugged her. The only lead he had was this guy, Adam Shepard. A long shot if there ever was one. As he drove past the guy's apartment building, he kept an eye out for the Spark, but he didn't see it. He did notice, however, that there were plenty of people milling around. Several families with kids. A couple of older guys walking down the sidewalk chatting.

It felt wrong. No way would the arsonist bring Jayme here, especially after drugging her. How would he get her inside past all these people without someone noticing? No, he'd take her somewhere else. Someplace private. Where no one would see or hear anything suspicious.

But where? Did this guy have another lair somewhere close by?

Or had he taken Jayme to her house?

Yes! He cranked the wheel, making an abrupt U-turn. The more he thought about the possibility of Jayme being held in her own house, the more desperate he felt to get there.

Please, Lord, don't let me be too late!

Driving like a madman, he made it to her house in less than ten minutes, each second feeling like an eternity. He drove past the place first, scanning it intently. There was no sign of the Spark, but maybe Shepard had ditched it after bringing Jayme here.

The house appeared empty. The garage door was closed, the curtains drawn. He made a quick turn, then pulled off to park along the side of the road. Time was of the essence; he needed to know if Jayme was there or not.

He reached over to grab his gun from the glove box, a weapon he'd never once been forced to use in the line of duty, before sliding out from behind the wheel.

Staying down, Linc ran lightly toward the garage. When he'd passed Jayme's house, he'd noticed the garage window wasn't covered with curtains or blinds. Peering inside, his pulse spiked when he saw the blue Chevy Spark.

He ducked back down and pulled out his phone. He called the 911 operator.

"This is Arson Investigator Lincoln Quade. I'm requesting police back up to this address." He rattled it off. "I have reason to believe Ms. Jayme Weston is being held inside against her will. The police need to know this is likely a hostage situation."

The operator repeated the address. "Is this correct?"

"Yes," he hissed. "Hurry."

"Please stay on the line," the operator said in a calm voice.

"No. Get Captain Barstow on the phone. He'll understand what I'm talking about." Linc didn't bother waiting for an answer. He disconnected from the call and pocketed his phone before slowly creeping along the side of the garage to the back of the house.

The last thing he wanted to do was shock Shepard into doing something hasty. Linc had to assume the guy had fuel of some sort to start a fire. That maybe this was his big finale, setting Jayme's house ablaze with her trapped inside.

Which meant there wasn't time to wait for backup either.

He made his way around the house, peering through every single window, even those with curtains. Upon reaching the back door, he found it locked.

Hesitating, he considered his options. Break in through the back? Go around to the front?

Bowing his head, he prayed for wisdom and strength.

Lord, guide me!

Taking a deep breath, he visualized the interior of the house. The garage door led into the kitchen. The kitchen and living area were combined into one open space. The back door opened into the laundry room, which wasn't far from the kitchen.

Shepard probably wouldn't have lugged Jayme's drugged body through the house. Based on the information from his driver's license, he was only five feet ten inches tall and one hundred and seventy pounds. No, Shepard would have only taken her as far as necessary.

Likely to the kitchen and/or living room.

Linc continued moving around the house, checking each of the windows to see if any were unlocked. He paused when he found one of Jayme's bedroom windows unlocked.

Without hesitation, he used a penknife to slice through the screen, then slowly lifted the inside window. Thankfully, it didn't make any noise. Seconds later, he'd shimmied through the opening, twisting and turning until his shoulders made it through.

The scent of kerosene hit hard. Fearing the worst, he moved swiftly to the door and peered out into the hall.

"You're not going to get away with this," Jayme was saying. "No matter what you do to me, Linc will hunt you down."

"I'll be long gone before that happens." The hoarse voice didn't sound at all familiar to him.

"You're getting kerosene all over your shoes," Jayme continued. "Aren't you worried you'll start on fire too? As I recall, you didn't appreciate that the last time."

Linc slipped down the hall, trying to get a bead on Shepard.

Click.

The sound was soft, barely audible. Linc caught his breath when he realized the sound had been a lighter.

"No!" Jayme screamed.

Linc darted out of the hallway. He saw Shepard

standing near the front door, holding the lighter and a wet rag. The pungent odor of kerosene was so strong Linc realized the guy had already spread it all over the floor.

A spark, either from the lighter or his gun, would ignite the entire area in flames.

Before he could shoot, the Preacher bent down and set the flame against the rag he'd soaked with kerosene. Instantly, fire erupted, spreading fast.

Linc fired at Shepard, but the guy had already disappeared through the door.

"Help me!" Jayme's frantic plea had him spinning toward her. The fire had spread all the way across the floor to her chair.

Linc tossed his gun and rushed forward, ignoring the heat of the fire biting at his ankles. With a herculean strength, he lifted Jayme and the chair off the floor and made a run for it down the hall toward the bedrooms.

"We're on fire, we're on fire," Jayme sobbed. Then she managed to get her hands free. "Put me down!"

He dropped the chair with enough force that the legs broke. He shrugged off his jacket and used it to douse the flames around her feet and his. Then he darted into the bathroom, ran the water in the sink over a towel. He tossed it to Jayme. "Use this on your feet."

"What about you?" She was already using the wet towel to smother the flames. Then she stripped off her shoes, socks, and jeans.

He doused a towel to use for himself, although the fire hadn't penetrated his shoes. His clothing hadn't started on fire either. Shepard had purposefully doused her feet and her jeans to draw the fire up and over her.

They had to get out of there. Linc needed to help find and catch this guy.

"How did you find me?" Jayme asked.

"Later." The air was thick with smoke. "We need to get out of here." He looked down at her feet. "Can you walk?"

"I think so." She coughed and winced as if her feet were tender and painful. But she hurried from the hallway into her bedroom, stopping long enough to grab another pair of jeans and shoes. He wanted to argue that modesty wasn't as important as getting out of the house, but she simply tossed the items out the window and began to climb out.

Linc glanced over his shoulder, his gaze landing on the bright orange light illuminating from the living room and kitchen area. The fire was clearly growing bigger, the greedy flames sucking up the accelerant. Then he turned and quickly followed Jayme outside, gratefully gulping the fresh air.

She sat on the grass, pulling on her jeans. He knelt beside her, raking his gaze over her legs and feet. "Are you okay? How badly are you burned?"

"I'm okay. My feet aren't as bad as I thought." She winced again as she rose to pull her jeans up over her hips. "You got me out of there just in time."

"Those burns need attention," he said firmly.

"I know." She stared at her reddened and already blistering feet. "I don't think I can put my shoes on after all."

Without hesitation, he swept her into his arms and carried her around to the front of the house, moving as fast as possible. He wanted her feet to get medical attention as soon as humanly possible.

Relief flooded over him when he saw several police squads along with a firetruck had just pulled up to her house.

"I need an ambulance," he shouted. "There's kerosene all around the main living area."

"Where's the firebug?" the fire captain asked.

"He got away." Linc felt like a failure for letting Shepard slip away. Yet saving Jayme's life had been far more important.

"Anyone else inside?"

"No, it's empty." Linc glanced down at Jayme who was staring at the fire eating away the interior of her home. "I'm sorry I didn't get here quicker."

She shook her head, her gaze still zeroed in on the fire. Finally, she turned to look up at him. "You were in time to save my life, that's what matters."

His heart squeezed painfully in his chest. Before he could say anything, two EMTs rushed toward them, pushing a gurney loaded with supplies.

"What happened?" one of them asked.

"Her feet and ankles have been burned." He waited for the EMTs to move the equipment so he could place her on the gurney. "I want you to take her to the Covenant Medical Center right away."

One EMT connected Jayme to a heart monitor as the other began soaking gauze with sterile water to place over her blisters. "They may want to transfer her to a burn unit at the university hospital," one of them warned.

"Whatever she needs." Linc forced himself to stay back, allowing them the room they needed to care for her.

"Linc? What about Caitlyn?" Jayme asked as the EMTs began to wheel her away.

He jogged alongside, doing his best to memorize her features. He knew she wasn't hurt badly, but he couldn't seem to stop himself. "She's safe with Devon."

"Thank you . . ." Her voice trailed off as the EMTs reached the ambulance. Minutes later, she was slid into the back, out of view.

Linc bowed his head as the ambulance whisked her away.

Thank you, Lord, for giving me the strength to save her.

JAYME IGNORED the pain in her feet, although it wasn't easy. When she closed her eyes, the image of the Preacher's evil smile popped into her mind, so she quickly opened them again. Staring up at the roof of the ambulance.

She'd felt certain she was going to burn to death. Had tried everything she could think of to convince the Preacher not to start the fire.

Even though she'd known there was no reaching him. He didn't have a soul, probably because he'd been possessed by the devil.

It was the only explanation as to why he'd delighted in the thought of burning her alive.

And the worst thing of all was that he'd gotten away. Why, oh, why hadn't she realized who he was sooner?

The ambulance hit a bump in the road that made her wince. Her feet had initially felt better being covered by the wet gauze, but the pain was getting worse and worse.

While she was thankful it hadn't been worse, she still couldn't understand why she had to suffer. What sins had she committed that she apparently still needed to atone for?

Hadn't she grown up the night of the fire? The night they'd made their escape? After getting all the foster kids out of the cabin, she'd taken Caitlyn under her wing and had dedicated herself to protecting the little girl.

The way no one in her life had protected her.

Their journey through the Smoky Mountains had been long and arduous. Hampered by her burned hand, the trek had seemed to take forever. They'd scrounged for food, had managed to kill several small rabbits, and had sheltered in the caves, then made do with camping in the woods by using leafy branches to shield themselves from the elements.

When they'd reached the city, they'd still struggled to survive. She'd stolen money, begged for food, and eventually managed to get a job.

She'd come so far that she never imagined the Preacher would catch up to her.

Attempting several times to kill her.

Tears slipped from the corners of her eyes. She lifted her hand to swipe them away.

Pull yourself up and step away from the pity party, she told herself sternly. Ruminating on the past, or on what might have happened, wasn't productive.

Linc had gotten there in time.

She was alive. That was something to be thankful for.

The ambulance pulled up to the hospital. Her pulse spiked. She could literally watch her heartbeat going faster and faster on the heart monitor. She took several deep breaths in an attempt to calm herself as the EMTs pulled her from the back of the ambulance and wheeled her inside.

"Vitals are stable, but she's sustained second-degree burns on her feet and ankles," one of the EMTs called out.

A slew of white coats surrounded her. "Give her something for pain," a man with a deep voice said.

"Wait." She reached out to grasp his hand. "I was drugged by the man who started the fire. I don't know what he gave me."

The kind eyes softened. "We'll run a tox screen, but there may not be enough time to wait for the results. We need to examine the extent of your injury. Try not to worry, burns are painful, so we'll give you just a little something to help you through this."

It was irrational, but she was afraid if they knocked her out, she'd never wake up. Silly because it wasn't as if burned feet could actually kill her.

No, if she was going to die, it would have been from being frightened to death by the Preacher.

The lights overhead grew fuzzy, the voices around her fading to mumbled sounds.

Then darkness overwhelmed her.

When Jayme awoke, she had no idea where she was. She lay frozen, her senses trying to make sense of the anti-septic smell, the beeping and hushed voices. Opening her eyes, she looked around, surprised to see an IV machine next to her bed.

And white bandages covering her feet and ankles.

The hospital. Memories cascaded over her. The Preacher, the kerosene, and the fire.

Linc lifting her and the chair up and out of the kitchen. The way she'd wrenched her hands free, scraping the skin raw. Climbing out her bedroom window, far too aware of how she was wearing nothing more than her underwear.

Linc lifting her in his arms, cradling her close as he carried her to the ambulance.

Being brought to the hospital for treatment of her burns.

Jayme's mouth was dry, her throat scratchy. Her hair reeked of smoke and kerosene, but when she looked down at herself, she was wearing a hospital gown, not her regular clothes.

She didn't like knowing someone had undressed her, but she told herself to get over it. She looked at her bandaged feet, surprised they didn't hurt.

God is taking care of you.

She actually looked over to see who was talking, but no one was there.

A tad eerie, yet at the same time, a strange sense of peace washed over her. She was going to be okay. Considering the pain she'd experienced when her hand had been burned, the wounds to her feet must be mild in comparison.

She was safe. Healthy. Alive.

Yet, she wished Linc was there, and Caitlyn too. She patted the bedding on either side of her, but there was no sign of her cell phone.

A ripple of unease washed over her. Pathetic as it sounded, being alone in the room without her cell phone felt a bit like being lost in a storm at sea. Ridiculous, really, since she hadn't been able to afford a regular cell phone until Remy Edgar had left her the money for their education.

Before that, she'd used a disposable one.

She almost hit the call button to summon the nurse but managed to stop herself. There was nothing the nurse could do for her. She wasn't in pain, her IV wasn't beeping, although someone's in the hallway was, and she couldn't borrow a phone because she didn't know Linc's phone number.

Then she saw the phone sitting on a small square nightstand, out of reach. Pushing herself up onto her elbows, she leaned over and snagged the phone.

Caitlyn's number she knew by heart, so she punched in the numbers. Unfortunately, her sister didn't answer.

"Cait? It's Jayme. Hey, just wanted to let you know I'm doing fine. Um, I don't have my phone, so I'll try you back later." She replaced the phone in its cradle.

Weird that her sister hadn't answered.

She stared up at the ceiling, doing her best not to panic.

Linc had said Caitlyn was with Devon. Given the change in Devon's demeanor after the GPS had been placed on Caitlyn's car and the cabin found and hit with a firebomb, she felt certain the young officer would do everything in his power to keep her sister safe.

Yet remembering how the Preacher had slipped out of the house made her shiver. He shouldn't have gotten away.

Then again, it was her own fault for letting him drug her up outside the clinic. She'd been fooled by his shuffling walk, the scar on his face that hadn't looked like a burn scar. Even his name. The fact that he'd been stronger than he'd looked made her realize he very well could have been the man in black running away from Sampson's that night.

Looking back, she wondered if part of the reason she hadn't paid him much attention was because he hadn't been her patient. Sandra had been the one following him, and the PT assistant had been a guy named Roger. How long had Shepard been coming to the clinic? Had to be at least four months.

Four months of seeing her, following her, spying on her while planning and plotting his revenge.

A plan that had almost succeeded.

He'd even come to the food pantry. That should have tipped her off, but it hadn't. Mostly because the man she'd thought of as Mr. Shepard had seemed to be the kind of man who needed food from the pantry.

But he'd only come in there because of her.

She pushed the thoughts away, reminding herself she couldn't go back and change the past.

A knock at her door drew her attention. "Come in," she called.

A pretty dark-haired nurse poked her head in. "Just checking to see how you're doing."

"I'm fine. My feet don't hurt at all." She frowned. "How bad are they?"

"Not as bad as they'd originally feared," the nurse said frankly. She took a few steps into the room. "My name is Renee, and I'll be your nurse until seven thirty. I learned in the report that the team in the ER used a burn cream to cover the wounds. The plan is to change the dressings around your feet and ankles twice a day."

Jayme automatically glanced at the clock. "I assume that's six thirty in the evening? Not in the morning?"

"Yes, in the evening. You were brought up to your room about ninety minutes ago." Renee crossed over to run her gaze over the IV pump. "Is there anything you need?"

"Ice water, if it's allowed."

"Oh, sure. Clear liquids are allowed, but nothing more yet. I'll be right back." Renee disappeared, returning a few minutes later with ice water.

Nothing had ever tasted so good.

"As long as I'm here, I'll need to check your vitals. Give me a minute to find a computer." Renee disappeared again, returning with a computer mounted to a wheeled cart. She opened the computer, then typed a bit before going on to check her blood pressure, pulse, and respiration.

Jayme wished she could see her chart. "I hate to ask, but the doctor in the ER told me he'd do a toxicology test because I'd been drugged by the man who started the fire. Can you give me the results?"

"Really? How awful." Renee looked horrified. "Yes, I see a tox screen was done, looks like it was positive for benzodiazepines."

"For what?"

"It's medications like Valium." Renee frowned. "I'm sorry to hear you were drugged by someone."

Jayme grimaced. "I'll be fine. But one last question before you go, any idea when I should expect the next dressing change?"

"I'm not sure about that one." Renee tapped the computer screen. "Dr. Sharma put the orders in, but I haven't seen anything about the next dressing change. I'm sure he'll be in later to discuss the treatment plan."

Jayme smiled. "Okay, thanks."

"Call if you need anything."

After the nurse left, Jayme tried to relax. She stared up at the TV hanging on the wall but didn't bother to turn it on. She'd never watched any television and wasn't sure she wanted to start now.

She must have dozed off again because a strange sound startled her. She blinked, assuming the doctor had arrived.

But the man who entered her room was wearing an eye patch and a face mask. The Preacher? How had he known where she was?

Jayme hit the call light, then jumped out of bed, ignoring the pain in her feet as she stood.

This time, she wasn't going to let him touch her.

Never again!

CHAPTER FOURTEEN

Linc ran his hands through his hair, swallowing a wave of frustration. Where was Shepard? His face had been plastered all over every single squad in the police force, and a BOLO—a be on the lookout—for him had been issued so that every officer would be on high alert.

He'd requested officers to be staked out in the front and back of Shepard's apartment building too. Linc had gone as far as to check his house, unwilling to put anything past this guy.

Still, there had been no sign of him.

Linc didn't like the fact that Shepard had gotten away in the first place, although there was nothing else he could have done. Jayme's feet and ankles had been burned despite his efforts to rescue her from the fire.

According to the hospital, her burns weren't as bad as he'd originally feared. He'd claimed to be her fiancé in order to get information from the doc. He'd be there now, except he was determined to find Shepard.

Deep down, he couldn't deny how much he liked the

idea of Jayme being his fiancée. Which was crazy because he'd sworn an oath to never replace Gina and Melody.

God had clearly put him in this situation for a reason. Linc had assumed his role was to bring Jayme to God, to heal the emotional wounds the Preacher had inflicted upon her. Yet they'd grown close over the past few days.

More than close.

She'd kissed him. And now he wanted nothing more than to pull her into his arms and kiss her again. He'd told himself the circumstances of their relationship had been heightened by the never-ending danger. The ongoing and escalating attacks against her.

Against both of them.

How would she feel about him once things had gone back to normal? Did they even have that much in common? He wasn't sure. Maybe once her feet had healed, they could go out for dinner, maybe see a movie.

Go out on a real date.

He drove to the hospital and parked in the surface lot. He texted Devon who reported everything was quiet at the hotel. The girls were watching movies, although Caitlyn continued to ask about Jayme. Linc had insisted that Caitlyn stay with Devon until they caught the Preacher.

Linc sent a message stating he was heading up to her room now to check on her and would report back. Devon had sent the a-okay emoji.

He smiled as he pushed out of the driver's side door. Staying away from the hospital had been incredibly difficult. He'd wanted to stay, to watch over Jayme, but his primary focus had been to help the Sevierville police track down Adam Shepard a.k.a. Simon Penske, a.k.a. the Preacher.

His goal had been to bring Jayme good news of the guy's

arrest. Unfortunately, he was coming empty-handed. He strode into the hospital and asked at the front desk about which room Jayme was in.

"Take the elevator to the third floor and head to the right," the woman instructed. "Room 320 is right at the end of the hallway."

"Got it, thanks." The directions were easy to follow. As he stepped off the elevator, he heard the dinging of a call light and a muffled cry, followed by a loud crash.

Jayme!

Linc barreled into room 320 and gaped in surprise at the man in scrubs who was stretched out on the floor beneath an IV pump. It took only a second for him to realize the guy was Shepard.

"I'm so glad you're here," Jayme gasped as she collapsed onto the bed, wincing in pain. "He just waltzed right into my room, holding a syringe. I think he decided to just kill me outright rather than trying to set another fire."

"Looks like you fought back," he said with grim satisfaction. There was a large, jagged wound on the top of Shepard's head from the edge of the IV pump that was bleeding profusely. He couldn't garner much sympathy for the guy.

"I—wasn't going to let him get close. Not like last time." She let out a shuddering breath. "I didn't realize who he was outside the clinic until he grabbed my elbow and did that weird curl around the bone with his index finger the way he did thirteen years ago." She shivered. "Before I could react, though, he drugged me. But not this time. I can't even explain how I was able to swing that IV pump at him. It wasn't heavy at all."

Linc took a moment to find ties to restrain Shepard's arms behind his back and to check for a pulse before crossing over to her. Shepard was still alive, but Linc didn't call for more help. Instead, he sat on the edge of her bed and draped an arm around her shoulders. "I'm sorry he got in here, Jayme. I have the entire police force looking for him, but I figured his goal was to escape. Not to double back here in an attempt to finish you off."

She leaned against him as if suddenly weary. "I didn't expect to see him either. I . . . knew he was obsessed with me, but this?" She shook her head. "I couldn't believe it when he showed up."

A nurse rushed into the room, gaping in horror at the body on the floor. "What happened?"

"He tried to kill me, so I hit him in the head with the IV pole." Jayme's voice was still hoarse, likely from the smoke from the fire.

"He's not dead, but you'll need a gurney to take him down to the emergency department." Keeping his arm around Jayme, he used one hand to call Captain Barstow. "Shepard is here at the hospital, he tried to attack Jayme."

"I'll send two squads there right away," Barstow said.

"No rush," Linc drawled. "Jayme hit him in the head with an IV pump."

"Really? Wow, that's amazing. I'm glad she was able to do that, he deserves it," Barstow chortled.

"No kidding." He leaned down and pressed a kiss to the top of Jayme's head. He knew it was wrong to be glad Shepard was hurt, but he couldn't help feeling satisfied at how Jayme had taken him down. "She's strong, and this time he'll pay for his crimes. They'll take him to the ER for care, his head is bleeding like a sieve, but I want officers sitting on him twenty-four seven the entire time he's here. We cannot allow him to escape again."

"Done," Barstow agreed. "I'll have the officers meet you down there."

"Okay." He disconnected from the call. The nurse who'd come to check in on them returned with a gurney. Linc didn't want to leave Jayme's side, but he forced himself to ease away. "I need to help them."

Jayme gave a jerky nod. "I know."

He removed the ties around Shepard's wrists and assisted with lifting him up and onto the gurney. Then he shackled one wrist to the gurney. "This stays in place until the officers arrive, understand?"

The nurse looked uneasy. "The doctor won't like it."

"Too bad. He's wanted for numerous crimes, including arson, kidnapping, and attempted murder." Linc drilled her with a narrow glare. "He looks helpless, but no matter what he tells you, don't believe it. He's a very dangerous man."

The nurse blanched. "Okay, so you're coming down to the ER with us, right?"

He needed to, but he glanced at Jayme. Her feet were up on the bed now, and he wondered if she'd injured herself worse because of this. "Yeah, I'm coming with you. Just give me a minute." He returned to her side, gazing down at her.

"I know you have to go." Jayme's smile didn't quite reach her eyes. "I understand. At least we know he won't hurt anyone else ever again."

"Jayme." He lifted her chin, encouraging her to meet his gaze. "I'll be back up here as soon as the officers arrive to relieve me, okay? You won't be alone for long."

"I know. I'll be fine."

He wanted nothing more than to pull her close and kiss her, but with the staff in the hallway and Shepard lying on the hospital gurney, this wasn't the time or the place to tell her what was in his heart.

He forced himself to take a step backward. "I'll be back soon," he repeated huskily.

She nodded, this time a real smile curling the corners of her mouth. "Thank you, Linc. For everything."

Her gratitude was like a kick to his gut because he'd failed her more often than not. He'd managed to get her out of the fire, but everything else she'd accomplished had been on her own. She'd been forced to smack Shepard in the head with an IV pump because he'd underestimated the guy.

Linc turned and followed the hospital staff who were pushing the gurney to the elevator. The trip down to the ER didn't take long, and soon the medical team was shouting orders as they cared for Shepard's head injury.

Linc stood back and watched. Shepard was starting to wake up, which likely meant he'd survive long enough to spend the rest of his life in prison.

He was okay with that.

"We need to get him into the CT scanner," one doc said in a loud tone. "We need to make sure he doesn't have internal bleeding into his brain."

"The scanner is ready, but the shackles need to come off." One of the nurses looked at him. "You need to release him."

"Not happening." Linc stepped forward. "I'll go with him to the scanner, and then release him long enough to get him moved into the machine."

The doc muttered something uncomplimentary beneath his breath.

"This man tried to start a woman on fire." His tone was sharp. "He'll remain in police custody until he's stable enough for jail, is that understood?"

A hush fell over the room as that information hit home. The doc nodded. "Fine. Keep him shackled."

Linc followed the gurney down the hall to radiology. He

removed the cuffs long enough for Shepard to be placed on the table, then he replaced them. He was soon joined by two police officers, Simons and Hill.

He gave them a nod. "Looks like you're pulling some overtime duty."

"We volunteered," Hill said. "This guy is a menace to society."

"Yeah, and it's bad enough Ms. Weston had to be the one to bring him down," Simons added. "The least we can do is keep him in custody."

"Thanks," Linc said, meaning it. The cops he'd worked with were great guys, from Captain Barstow all the way down the line.

Which reminded him of Devon. Linc needed to report in, very soon. But he didn't want to do that without checking in to see if Jayme's feet were okay.

"I'm heading upstairs to sit with Jayme," he told them. "Don't let Shepard out of your sight."

"We won't," Hill assured him. Then he frowned and added, "Will Ms. Weston be all right?"

"Yes, she'll be fine." At least he hoped she hadn't injured her feet worse while fighting off Shepard. He nodded at the two men, then quickly returned to the elevator, tapping his foot impatiently as he made his way to the third floor.

Her door was open, but he rapped on it anyway. "Jayme? It's Linc, can I come in?"

"Yes."

Upon entering the room, he noticed Captain Barstow standing there. Barstow turned toward him. "I was just following up with Ms. Weston, apologizing for the way Shepard managed to get in here."

"I told him you'd already apologized for that," Jayme

said. Her expression looked weary, as if she'd used all her strength to fight off Shepard. "I'm just glad he's in custody."

"You're an amazing woman, Ms. Weston," Barstow said.

Linc squelched the flash of jealousy. Jayme deserved every bit of respect she'd won from the police department.

And more.

Once Barstow left, he crossed the room to sit in the chair beside her. "How are your feet?" he asked.

"Fine." Jayme shrugged. "The doc stopped in to change the bandages, told me that standing up for that short amount of time didn't cause any long-term damage."

"I'm relieved to hear that." He reached out and took her hand, for his peace of mind more than hers.

"I tried to call Caitlyn, but she didn't answer." Jayme glanced at him. "She's okay, right?"

"I spoke to Devon right before I came up to see you. He told me Caitlyn and Annette were watching movies." He handed her his phone. "Go ahead and call her."

She entered the number and lifted the phone to her ear. "Caitlyn? Are you okay?"

Linc couldn't hear the other part of the conversation but became alarmed when he noticed her tears.

"When you didn't answer the phone earlier, I panicked," Jayme said. "I guess I should have figured you wouldn't answer an unknown number."

Linc made a mental note to track down her cell phone. The hospital must have stashed her belongings somewhere.

"I'm fine, especially now that the Preacher has been arrested. You don't have to worry about him ever again, Cait."

The guy had targeted Jayme, not her sister, but he understood Jayme's concern. He'd been worried the guy would go after Caitlyn as a surrogate too.

Never again.

Jayme swiped at her face as she handed him the phone. "Thanks. I was going crazy here without being able to talk to anyone."

"I understand, but you won't be alone anymore. I'm staying here until you're released."

Her blue eyes widened. "Oh, I'm not sure that's necessary, Linc. I know you still have things to do."

"Nothing as important as this," he insisted.

"I'm safe now that the Preacher has been arrested." She stared at her bandaged feet. "Sounds like I'll be discharged by tomorrow anyway. No need for you to stay here all night."

He frowned, trying to understand what she was telling him. "You don't want me to stay with you?"

"I—um, it's not that." Jayme rubbed at the scar on her hand, a gesture he'd come to realize meant she was nervous. "I don't want you to feel obligated. I'm not in danger anymore. You have your life, Linc, and I need to get back to mine."

Her house was a crime scene, not to mention fire and water damaged, but he sensed she was talking about the two of them.

"I appreciate everything you've done for me," she went on. "You've been wonderful to me and Caitlyn."

It sounded a lot like she was telling him goodbye. And while he was the one who'd told her there couldn't be anything more than friendship between them, everything that had transpired in the past few hours had changed his mind about that.

He cared about her, had even fallen in love with her.

But that didn't mean she felt the same way about him.

JAYME WAS HOLDING herself together with a string and a prayer. She knew Linc wasn't interested in a relationship and had given him the perfect opportunity to leave.

"Truly, I'm fine," she said, trying to convince herself just as much. "You don't have to stay and play babysitter."

"What if I want to stay?" Linc leaned forward and grasped her hand. Her fingers automatically curled around his. "I care about you, Jayme. I only left you alone so I could try to find Shepard. We found his apartment, and I arranged officers to stake the place out in case he returned."

That bit of information surprised her. "He had an apartment?"

"Near the physical therapy clinic." Linc held her gaze. "The moment I knew you were missing, I did everything possible to find you. Even convincing the clinic therapists, Sandra and Jake, to give me a list of their clients."

"But that's confidential information!" Jayme couldn't help being shocked by what Sandra and Jake had done.

"Your life was on the line, Jayme." He didn't show any remorse, and deep down, she was glad Sandra and Jake had cooperated with him. She just hoped they wouldn't get into trouble over it. "And it worked because the moment I saw Adam K. Shepard's name, I sensed he was the one. When I looked him up in the DMV database, the scar on his face was wrong, but I was still convinced."

"The scar was fake; he used a rubbery putty-like substance to cover up his burn scars." She shook her head. "I should have realized he was the Preacher. Although in my defense, I truly thought he was dead."

"I know." Linc lifted her scarred hand and kissed it.

"I'm so glad I found you, Jayme. I only wish I'd gotten there earlier."

"I kept him talking in an attempt to stall for time. I was hoping Mrs. Katz would notice something was off and call the police." She was amazed at how easily he accepted her burn-ravaged hand when others had shunned the scars. "And I prayed, Linc, in a way I've never prayed before."

"I know God was guiding me to you." His gaze bored into hers. "I'm only sorry it took me so long to rescue you. But I didn't dare shoot, not the way he was holding that lighter . . ."

"It's okay. I completely understand," she hastened to assure him.

"Jayme. I was so afraid I was going to lose you." Linc's voice was so low she could barely hear him.

"It's my fault, Linc. I'm the one who insisted on helping out at the clinic." She hated seeing him so racked with guilt. "I don't blame you at all. I accept the consequences of my actions." A smile tugged at the corner of her mouth. "But I still prayed you'd find me in time. And you did."

"I love you."

She stared at him, wondering if she'd said those words or if he did. She didn't think she'd said them out loud.

"I love you, Jayme Weston," he repeated.

"But—your wife and daughter . . ." She trailed off, struggling to find a way to express her doubts. "I know they still own your heart."

"They did, yes," Linc admitted. "There's a part of me that will always love them. But they're in a much better place now, and God has kept me on earth because my work isn't done yet."

So he saw her as part of his work? It made sense, and she tried to ignore the shaft of disappointment. "But you don't have to protect me anymore. I'm safe now that the Preacher has been arrested. And so is Caitlyn."

"Yes, I know." He frowned. "My attempt to keep you at a professional distance failed miserably. I fell in love with you. And I can understand if you don't feel the same way, but I hope you'll give me a chance."

Maybe the smoke and kerosene had made her brain mush because she didn't understand how he'd gone from the fact that his work wasn't done to claiming he loved her. "Linc, we've been through a lot over the past few days."

"Look, Jayme. I love you." He looked impatient now. "I love you, and I want to spend time with you. Will you at least allow me to take you out for dinner?" He glanced guiltily at her bandaged feet. "Once you're healed."

"I'd love to have dinner, but I don't want you to think of me as some sort of project you need to fix."

"I don't." He fell silent for a moment, then nodded. "Okay, I'm an idiot."

She burst out laughing. "I didn't say that."

"When I said God has a plan for me, that my work wasn't done here, I meant that God wanted me to find you, Jayme. That God brought us together."

Understanding dawned. "You really love me?"

"I can't think of any more ways to say it," he admitted. "I love you, and I want to be with you. I hope you'll give me that chance."

"Oh, Linc." She couldn't help but smile. "Of course, I'll go out with you, because I love you too."

"Praise God," he said reverently. Then he jumped up to sit beside her, drawing her carefully into his arms. "I'd like to kiss you," he whispered.

"I'd like that too." She reached up and drew his head

down to hers. Her heart soared at the mix of tenderness and passion in his kiss.

"Um, Jayme?" A female voice from the doorway made her break off from Linc's embrace. When she saw Caitlyn standing there, with Devon and Annette behind her, she wanted to groan.

She loved her sister, but couldn't she have waited a few more minutes? Maybe an hour? Or two?

"Sorry to interrupt." Devon shot an apologetic glance at Linc. "But Caitlyn insisted on coming, and after hearing the news that Shepard was in custody, I figured she had a right to see her sister."

"Jayme, I've been so worried." Caitlyn stepped closer. "You sounded upset during our earlier call."

"It's all been a bit overwhelming," Jayme admitted. "But as you can see, I'm fine."

"How long will your feet need to be bandaged?" Caitlyn asked.

"A few weeks, but they're only first- and second-degree burns." Jayme smiled. "The doc mentioned something about the shoes melting around my feet from the fire, which didn't help. I'm blessed the injuries weren't worse."

"I can't believe the Preacher didn't die in the cabin," Caitlyn said. "All this time, we assumed he was dead."

"He escaped out the bedroom window and somehow managed to avoid all of us hiding in the woods."

"How did he find you?" Caitlyn asked.

"I'm thinking he knew Jayme's real last name and found her through the physical therapy clinic," Linc said. His comment made her wince. It had never occurred to her to change her name. "She's listed as an employee."

"But there's no need to worry," Jayme insisted. "He'll never hurt anyone again."

"I'm glad." Caitlyn's smile was lopsided. "I used to have nightmares about him."

"I know, me too." Caitlyn had suffered with the rest of the fosters for two years. As much as Jayme had tried to protect her, she couldn't erase all the memories from the past.

But she had done her best to provide new, happy memories.

"Hey, we should go back to the hotel so your sister can rest," Devon said.

"The hotel?" Jayme glanced at Linc. "The girls can probably head back to their apartment now that the danger is over."

"They could, but we already paid for the room." Linc shrugged. "Why not let them stay one more night? Devon can drive them to class in the morning."

"Okay."

Caitlyn came over to give her a hug, and Jayme held her tightly for a long moment.

Then they were gone, leaving her and Linc alone.

Exhaustion weighed on her, and she ended up falling asleep. The nursing staff checked on her throughout the night, and each time, Linc remained by her side. He gave her privacy when she needed to go into the bathroom but then resumed his position in the chair.

"You should go home and get some rest," she told him.

"Tomorrow, if you're discharged." He yawned. "Until then, I'm staying."

Stubborn man, she thought fondly.

The doc came in bright and early to do her dressing changes. She insisted on watching, although Linc had looked a little sick at seeing her injuries.

"They're looking good," the doc said. "I'll send you

home as long as you continue changing the bandages and putting on more burn cream twice a day."

"I can do that," Jayme agreed.

"I'll help," Linc bravely added.

"All right then, I'll put through the discharge paperwork." The doc smiled and left.

The entire process took longer than it should, so it was almost three hours later before Jayme was placed in a wheelchair and pushed outside.

Instantly, a mob of people rushed toward her. "Ms. Weston, Ms. Weston! How do you feel about the role you played in getting Mr. Shepard behind bars?"

Jayme glanced up at Linc. He winced. "Reporters," he said in a low voice. "You've been big news these past few days."

She looked around in shock. She'd had no idea. "I'm glad he'll spend the rest of his life behind bars," she said. "Now if you'll excuse me, I'd like to go home."

"Jayme?" A familiar voice caught her attention. She turned and felt as if she'd been punched in the chest when she saw a man that looked like a grown-up version of Sawyer.

Not just Sawyer, but all of them. A few feet from the reporters she saw them all. Hailey, Darby, Sawyer, Cooper, and Trent.

A rush of emotion hit hard. Her foster siblings were alive!

CHAPTER FIFTEEN

Linc tightened his grip on Jayme's wheelchair, but he needn't have worried. A group of young adults rushed toward Jayme who was crying and laughing at the same time.

"I can't believe you're all here," Jayme said as they all took turns hugging her. "How did you find me?"

"It wasn't hard the way your face has been plastered all over the news," a guy with short dark hair said wryly. "The moment we learned you were here, we all banded together to come and see you."

"Oh, Sawyer." Jayme sniffled. "I haven't watched any television, so I had no idea I was on the news."

Linc was impressed to hear Jayme's foster siblings had come all the way to Sevierville just to see her. It seemed they'd all found each other before and had only just now learned about Jayme. "Listen, we should get out of here, or the reporters will be all over us," he warned.

"Where's Caitlyn?" a woman with long, straight dark hair asked. "We thought for sure she'd be here."

"She lives here in Sevierville, Hailey, but she has class

today." Jayme glanced up at him. "This is Linc Quade, my, er . . ."

"Boyfriend," Linc supplied, secretly pleased when Jayme smiled, her cheeks turning red. The sooner she got used to hearing that, the better. "Listen, it's really great to meet all of you, but we really need to get away from here." The reporters were already watching the exchange with far too much interest. "Can you meet us at my place?" Linc rattled off the address.

Sawyer nodded. "Of course. We have our respective spouses with us so prepare for a crowd."

"Everyone is welcome," Linc said sincerely. "And we'll bring Caitlyn over from the college too."

"College," a woman with short blond hair said, putting a hand on a boy who was roughly five or six. "That's impressive."

"Darby, who is this adorable little boy?" Jayme smiled at the shy child.

"My son, Leo." Darby beamed. "I—well, it's a long story."

Linc had a feeling they all had a long story to tell. Including Jayme. "Let's go, okay?" He wanted to ditch the reporters and fast.

"Ms. Weston! How badly were you burned in the fire?" one woman shouted as Linc pushed Jayme's wheelchair to his rental.

"No comment," he said tersely. He quickly lifted Jayme up and into the passenger seat, then slammed the door, effectively cutting the reporters off. He quickly slid behind the wheel and headed out of the parking lot, narrowly missing one of the cameramen who had chosen to stay in the middle of the road to keep filming.

"I can't believe the fosters are here." Jayme appeared

dazed. "They all look so great, so grown up. I noticed Sawyer was wearing a wedding ring, and I think Darby was too. I didn't have time to check all of them, but they look happy and healthy."

"They did," he agreed. "Very much so."

"It's surreal to realize that after all these years we've found each other."

"God brought you together," Linc murmured. "As soon as we get to my place, I'll call Devon, ask him to bring Caitlyn over."

"Thank you." Jayme reached over to grasp his hand. "It was very sweet of you to offer your home as a meeting spot."

"Jayme, I don't want you to take this the wrong way, but I'd like you to stay with me while your house is being repaired. In the guest bedroom," he hastened to add. "I promise not to take advantage of the situation."

"Are you sure?" Doubt laced her tone.

"I'm sure." He wanted her to stay with him forever but refrained from saying the words. She'd barely admitted her feelings for him, he didn't want to overwhelm her too much.

"Okay, thanks. I look like a wreck," she said, threading her fingers through her hair.

"You're beautiful," he corrected. "Smart, brave, strong, and beautiful. Don't forget that for one moment."

"I'll try." She grimaced. "Although a shower would be nice."

"You can't get the bandages on your feet wet," he reminded her.

"I know."

He pulled into his driveway and quickly ran up to unlock the house. Everything appeared undisturbed since they'd left it last. Returning to the SUV, he swept Jayme into his arms and carried her inside.

"The doc said I could walk short distances," she protested.

"Yeah, like to the bathroom and back. All other walking is off-limits. The more you stay off your feet, the faster you'll heal."

Once he had Jayme settled on the sofa, he called Devon. "Where are you?"

"Just got out of the shower, I have to report in to work at three o'clock," Devon said. "Why? Did something happen? I thought you had Shepard in custody?"

"Everything is fine, he's in custody and still at the hospital. I need a favor. Would you be willing to pick Caitlyn up from school and bring her to my place?" Linc asked. He poked his head in the fridge, glad to see he had plenty of bottled water and soft drinks.

"Yes, but why?"

"All of her foster siblings have arrived in town." Linc closed the fridge. "She won't want to miss the impromptu reunion."

"Wow, she has other foster siblings aside from Jayme?" Devon sounded surprised. "She never mentioned them."

"Well, I get the sense Jayme and Caitlyn didn't talk about their past to anyone." Linc could tell the young man was hurt by the news that Caitlyn hadn't confided in him. "It's nothing personal, but as you know, the Preacher made their life a living nightmare."

"Yeah, he did," Devon agreed. "I'll head over to get her, but she may want to wait until her class is finished."

"The sooner the better," Linc said. "Trust me, she'll want to see them as much as they're anxious to see her."

"Got it." Devon disconnected from the call.

A car pulled behind his rental, followed by another. A caravan of four vehicles, as it seemed each foster sibling had brought a significant other with them. Two couples got out of one car, the rest had their own mode of transportation.

Linc went over to open his door. "Come in, make yourselves at home."

"Nice place," Hailey said with admiration. "Thanks for hosting us all at the last minute."

"Jayme's family is important to me," he replied honestly. "And Caitlyn should be here soon."

The group of people trooped inside, gathering around Jayme. Some sat on the furniture, but many sat on the floor to be closer to her.

Linc took another minute to order several large pizzas of all different kinds of toppings, along with more soft drinks, fearing he wouldn't have enough.

Then he hung back, content to watch and listen.

This was Jayme's moment. Her time to be with her family.

He was happy enough to be a part of this momentous occasion.

"JAYME, I'd like you to meet my wife, Naomi Palmer," Sawyer introduced her to a pretty blonde. "We live in Chattanooga."

"And this is my husband, Gage, and our son, Leo," Darby added. "We live in Knoxville."

"So close!" Jayme was surprised at the news. "And don't forget, you promised to tell me the story about that. Although I won't put you on the spot here in front of everyone."

"I don't mind." Darby turned and exchanged a smile

with her husband. "Everything we suffered through has only made us stronger in our faith, right, Gage?"

"Exactly right," he agreed. "We're blessed to be here, together as a family."

Jayme was touched by his words, but soon Cooper caught her attention.

"Jayme, this is my wife, Mia. We live in Knoxville now too." Cooper smiled lovingly at his wife. Jayme grinned at how handsome the guys were. Sawyer, Cooper, and Trent were all gorgeous without seeming to be aware of it.

"Nice to meet you, Mia." She turned toward Trent. "Don't tell me you're married too?"

"We're engaged," Trent corrected. "But I hope to marry Serena very soon. We live in Nashville." He held the pretty girl's hand. "I've told her all about you and Caitlyn. And the others, too, of course."

"Last but not least, this is my fiancé, Rock Wilson," Hailey said. "We're getting married in less than two weeks. I know you've been injured"—she glanced down with a slight frown at Jayme's bandaged feet—"but I hope you'll join us. We're getting married in a church in Gatlinburg, where we live."

"Gatlinburg is really close. I'd be happy to come." Jayme was surprised they'd all ended up in Tennessee. She glanced at Linc who stood in the kitchen watching them with a smile on his face. "That is if Linc doesn't mind accompanying me."

"I wouldn't miss it," he assured her. "Oh, and I've ordered pizzas and more soft drinks. You're welcome to have anything from the fridge."

"Could I bother you for some water?" Jayme's throat was still sore from the smoke she'd inhaled. She wanted to get up and walk over to get it herself, but not only was she surrounded by the fosters, she knew Linc wanted her to stay off her feet. She could already tell she was going to hate feeling like a burden.

"Of course." Linc pulled several water bottles out and passed them around. Hailey handed hers to Jayme, then took another.

Jayme sipped her water, wondering where to start. The fosters had a right to know about the Preacher.

"Caitlyn's here," Linc announced.

"Where's Annette?" Jayme asked as her sister came into the house.

"She stayed in class to take notes." Caitlyn looked surprised as everyone rose to their feet to welcome the youngest sibling with hugs.

Tears pricked at Jayme's eyes as she realized Gage was right about how blessed they were to be there together.

"Caitlyn, you look amazing," Hailey gushed. "So grown up! I'm not sure I would have recognized you on the street."

"I totally agree," Darby chimed in. "You're beautiful."

"You're here." Caitlyn's expression was dazed as she looked from one foster sibling to the other. "You're all here."

More introductions were made to include Caitlyn.

"I hope there's not a test." Caitlyn plopped down onto the sofa beside Jayme. "I'll fail for sure."

"No test," Jayme assured her. Then she turned to look at her foster family. That they'd come so far out of their way to visit was humbling. Her gaze turned serious. "I have some news to share. You should probably know the Preacher didn't die in the fire that night."

"What?" Sawyer's expression was shocked. "He must have died, I poisoned him and Ruth with pokeweed berries hidden in the blueberry pie."

"And I spilled moonshine all over the floor beneath their bed," Darby added.

"I brought in wet wood," Trent admitted. "Figured the smoke was part of the reason they never got out of the cabin."

"I spilled my oil paints and left them near my sketchbook," Cooper said. "I thought for sure that's how the fire grew out of control."

"Hold on," Jayme said, lifting her burned hand in the air. "I had no idea you all felt responsible for the fire, but it was me. I was the one who started it. The Preacher was trying to pin me down to, uh—well, it doesn't matter. I hit him with the oil lantern. The fire started on the sofa." She displayed her hand. "This is where I was burned that day."

The group fell silent, staring in shock.

"I never knew," Hailey whispered. "I smelled the smoke and woke the others, but I didn't realize you actually started the fire."

"Not on purpose," Jayme said somewhat defensively. "But yeah, I was desperate to get away." She glanced at Sawyer. "Pokeweed berries? No wonder Ruth stayed in her room."

"I didn't know the Preacher attacked you, Jayme." Sawyer's expression was grim. "I'm glad you started the fire, although I'm not happy you were burned. Still, the fire is the reason we escaped that night."

"That's true," Cooper added. The others nodded in agreement. "You saved our lives, Jayme. I'm just sorry you had to be burned while doing that."

"But I don't understand. How do you know the Preacher is still alive?" Darby asked, pressing a hand to her abdomen as if she felt sick. "Have you seen him?"

"Yes." Jayme stared at her feet for a moment. "He

taunted me by starting fires—my car, the physical therapy clinic where I work, Linc's car." She drew in a deep breath. "Then he drugged me and took me to my house. There, he tied me to a chair and tried to burn me alive."

"No!" Trent stared in horror. "That's terrible. I can't believe he found you after all this time!"

Jayme nodded. "Me either. Like you, I had assumed he was dead. Linc found his and Ruth's obituary."

"It was terrifying," Caitlyn added. "He was obsessed with seeking revenge on Jayme."

"I'm fine, though." Jayme glanced over to where Linc watched. "Linc saved my life. And don't worry, the Preacher has been found and placed in police custody." She smiled rather grimly. "The good news is that he'll spend the rest of his life in jail where he'll never hurt anyone ever again."

A heavy silence fell amongst the group as they digested this information.

"Praise God," Sawyer finally said.

"Yes, thank You, Lord," Hailey agreed.

Jayme was stunned as the rest of the fosters all joined in their praise to God. Not only had each of the fosters survived, but they'd also thrived. Had fallen in love, gotten married or engaged, and despite everything they'd been through, they'd become believers.

Well, except for Caitlyn, whom she'd barely had time to talk to about God. Still, the look on her youngest sister's face indicated she was open to the idea.

A warm joy spread through her. God really had been watching out for them. For all of them. God had brought Linc into her life when she needed him the most. Her gaze locked with Linc's across the room. He smiled, and as if he knew what she was thinking, he mouthed the words, "I love you."

"I love you too, Linc." she said loud enough for everyone to hear. "Very much."

"Yay!" Caitlyn clapped her hands. "I hoped you two would get together." Her youngest sister beamed. "I knew you would be perfect for each other."

Jayme smiled and shook her head in amazement as the others joined the celebration. "Cheers to Linc and Jayme," Cooper said, raising his water bottle.

The others lifted their water bottles in a toast. Their excitement only grew more frenzied when Linc announced the pizzas had arrived.

"Smells great," Trent said, rising to his feet and offering his hand to his wife.

"You can always eat," Serena teased, jabbing him with her elbow.

The group moved from Linc's living area into the kitchen. She was about to stand when Linc came over with a plate. "Don't move, I've got you covered."

"Oh, Linc." She took the plate and gazed up into his dark eyes. "I can't thank you enough. This is the best pizza party ever."

"Your family is incredible." He reached up to tuck a strand of her hair behind her ear. "The way you all triumphed over your past to find faith, hope, and love is amazing."

"It really is," she agreed. She set the plate aside and shifted toward him. "I love you, Lincoln Quade."

"And I love you, Jayme Weston." He lowered his head to hers, and she gladly kissed him.

When the entire room burst into applause, she broke off the kiss and shook her head ruefully. "How embarrassing."

"Never," Linc said in a husky voice. "They're happy for you, Jayme. For us."

"I know, it's just, it's all still so new." She glanced at him. "After taking care of me for a few weeks, you might change your mind."

"Not a chance." Linc didn't hesitate to kiss her again. "Have faith, Jayme. Our love will get us through, no matter what."

As Jayme soaked up the joy and laughter of her foster family surrounding them, she believed God's journey had brought her here to him.

EPILOGUE

Hailey's wedding day . . .

Linc pushed Jayme's wheelchair from the church into the gathering area where they would have a light lunch. "The ceremony was so wonderful," Jayme gushed.

"Hailey made a beautiful bride." He gazed down at Jayme, realizing he'd misspoke. This woman he loved with his whole heart would be a stunning bride.

"The only bummer is being stuck in this wheelchair." Jayme grimaced. "Sorry, I know I promised to stop complaining."

"You don't have to apologize to me, Jayme." He understood how frustrated she'd been with being restricted to a wheelchair. Being immobile and dependent on others wasn't easy, especially not for someone who'd been independent as long as Jayme had been. The good news was that her burned feet were healing nicely. At their last visit, the doc seemed to think she'd be able to walk on them by the end of the month.

"How are you feeling?" Darby came over to stand

beside them. Darby had been Hailey's matron of honor, her little boy, Leo, the ring bearer. Cooper had stood up as Rock's best man. Linc thought it was awesome how Hailey and Rock had included several of the fosters in their celebration.

And that they were all able to attend the wedding.

"I'm fine," Jayme assured her. "Leo did such a wonderful job as ring bearer."

"He was a star," Darby agreed with a smile. She glanced over at her husband who was chasing Leo. "Gage is a wonderful father."

Over the course of the reunion, he and Jayme had learned how several of the fosters had overcome their fears to fall in love. Hailey had tried to ditch Rock several times before accepting his help. Sawyer had convinced Naomi to trust him to help care for her younger sister. Darby had betrayed Gage to save herself and her unborn child, but Gage had won her back. Mia had tried to leave Cooper so that he wouldn't have to give up his newly found foster family. Serena had refused to give up on Trent, despite his issues with alcohol abuse.

They emulated the epitome of love and acceptance.

When they were all gathered together, each holding a glass of sparkling grape juice, Linc cleared his throat. "I know we're here today to celebrate Hailey and Rock, and I do want to congratulate the both of you on your new life together."

"Here, here," Trent shouted.

"But I hope you don't mind if I take a moment for Jayme," Linc pressed.

"Of course not," Hailey assured him. "We each owe our lives to her."

He nodded, suspecting most of the fosters would feel that way. He turned and dropped to one knee beside Jayme's wheelchair. He held up the diamond engagement ring that Caitlyn had helped him choose. "Jayme, will you please marry me?"

Jayme gaped in surprise, then flushed and laughed. "Yes, Linc. Yes, I'll marry you."

"Cheers to Jayme and Linc!" Cooper said, lifting his glass of sparkling grape juice.

"Yay, sis!" Caitlyn rushed over to give Jayme a hug. "I'm so happy for you both."

"Does this mean you'll invite us to your wedding?" Trent teased. "I really like these family reunions."

Darby laughed. "I can get on board with that plan."

"Me too," Hailey agreed. "Having all of you here today has made our wedding very special."

"Welcome to the family, Linc," Sawyer said. "We're happy to have you."

Linc smiled down at Jayme. This was God's plan for him, and as much as he missed Gina and Melody, he was truly blessed to be given a second chance at love. At a family. A much bigger family than he'd anticipated.

"How do you feel about a Christmas wedding?" he murmured to Jayme. "I'm thinking your feet will have healed by then. And there's no better time for another family reunion than right before the holidays."

"I love it," she whispered. "But not as much as I love you, Linc."

He kissed her. "I love you more." Now and forever.

THANK you so much for reading *Jayme's Journey*. I hope you enjoyed all the books in my Smoky Mountain Secrets series. If you're curious about Caitlyn's story, I've written a Christmas Novella to give her the happily ever after she deserves. If you'd like to read *Caitlyn's Christmas,* Click Here!

DEAR READER

Thanks again to all of you who took the time to let me know how much you've enjoyed this series. I wanted to write a series of stories about a group of kids who were bonded through tragedy and who rose above their awful past to find God and love.

If you enjoyed this story, please consider taking a moment to leave a review. Reviews are very important to authors, and I would really appreciate your kind gesture.

I'm truly blessed to have such wonderful readers! Please know I'd love to hear from you! I can be found on Facebook at https://www.facebook.com/LauraScottBooks, on Twitter at https://twitter.com/laurascottbooks, and on Instagram at https://www.instagram.com/laurascottbooks/. I can also be reached through my website at https://www.laurascottbooks.com. If you're interested in hearing about my new releases, consider signing up for my newsletter. You'll receive a free novella that is not available for purchase through any platform. It is exclusive only to my newsletter subscribers.

Lastly, this series wouldn't be complete if Caitlyn didn't also find love. Next month, I'll release *Caitlyn's Christmas*! I've included a sneak peek here.

Until next time,

Laura Scott

CAITLYN'S CHRISTMAS

Caitlyn Weston gasped and slammed on the brakes as a white animal streaked across the road. Wrenching her small car over onto the shoulder, she immediately pushed open her driver's side door to climb out, despite the blustery December wind.

The animal had been a small cat, and she was fairly certain she'd glimpsed blood marring the side of his or her coat. As a veterinary technician, she adored animals and couldn't bear the idea of this small cat being out in the cold, especially while injured. She glanced over her shoulder nervously as she quickly headed into the woods where the cat had disappeared. Her hometown of Sevierville, Tennessee, nestled near the Smoky Mountains, was only five miles away. Still, it was late, just after midnight, and the moon and the stars were hidden behind thick clouds.

"Here, kitty. Nice kitty." The white cat might be feral, although she found it strange that it would be running around this far out of town where it would be more likely to end up as a coyote's meal ticket.

"Kitty? Nice kitty?" she called again. Patches of snow

lingered from a storm a few days ago making it difficult to see the white cat.

There! Light-colored eyes winked at her from the darkness.

"Here, kitty." She wished she had food to entice the animal closer. While working at the veterinary clinic, she always had treats in her pockets. Tonight, though, she'd been out on a date, a failed experiment since Nate Powers, the guy she'd been with, had been far more interested in the female lead in the country-western band they'd gone to hear. She doubted he'd even noticed she'd left.

"I'm not going to hurt you," she murmured, edging closer. "I just want to help. You're cold and hungry, right? I can help you."

The cat blinked but didn't move. Caitlyn came a little closer, frowning when she realized the feline was shivering. She unwrapped the red scarf from around her neck and held it out. "Here, kitty. Do you want to warm up?"

She'd been told by Dr. John Vice, one of the veterinary docs at the clinic, that she had a voice animals responded well to. She continued inching toward the cat when the ball of fur stood and came over to nose the scarf.

Yes! Caitlyn slowly and carefully folded the other end of the red scarf around the cat. The feline burrowed into the scarf, seeking warmth and comfort.

Definitely not a stray, she thought as she gathered the cat and the scarf up from the ground. Cradling the animal to her chest, she wondered if the cat was microchipped as she turned to head back to her car.

A muffled scream stopped her dead in her tracks.

What was that?

Caitlyn turned, raking her gaze over the wooded area. Some wild animals could sound like people, especially while mating. Was that what she'd heard? She took another step when she heard a deep male voice.

"You're going to pay, not me!"

"No, please—"

A harsh slapping sound made her gasp. Caitlyn shivered as repressed memories of the time she lived with the Preacher flashed in her mind. The Preacher had slapped her across the face when one of the older foster kids had stood up to him in a way he deemed unacceptable. He'd liked using her as a pawn to control her older foster siblings.

But that was a long time ago. She was safe now.

Yet another woman wasn't.

She needed to do something. She had her phone, but she was worried the man might hear her make a 911 call. Maybe she could take him by surprise, give the woman enough time to get away. Yes, that was a good plan.

But first she had to find them.

Easing through the woods, she made her way toward the muffled sounds of someone struggling.

Movement between two thick trees caught her attention. The cat in her arms began to purr, making her wince. Was the sound loud enough to be heard by the arguing couple? She made her way through the brush as silently as possible. Where were they? Finally, she was close enough to see them. A tall man wearing a black coat was using his large hands to choke a woman with long dark hair. Her heart thundered in her chest as she watched in horror. How long had he held her like that? How long had it taken her to get through the woods? Too long. The woman's entire body was slack as he continued cutting off the circulation to her brain.

No! Caitlyn fumbled for her phone but then froze when the woman dropped in a crumpled heap to the ground.

Even from here, she could see the whites of the woman's open eyes, staring up at the dark sky. The man glared down at her for long moments, breathing heavily, before mumbling something under his breath and turning away.

Run!

Caitlyn sensed there was nothing she could do for the woman now. She'd been too late. The woman was dead.

And the man could easily kill her too.

Shrinking backward, she retraced her steps, trying to remember where she'd left her car. The sense of urgency propelled her forward, and she feared she was making too much noise. That the man who'd just murdered that poor woman would realize she'd seen him.

The cat in her arms was silent now, maybe realizing the precariousness of her position. Tossing a furtive glance over her shoulder, she nearly tripped over a log half hidden in a patch of snow.

When she burst through the trees, Caitlyn nearly sobbed in relief when she saw her small gray Honda. She ran toward it, yanking the door open and sliding in behind the wheel. Keeping the cat on her lap, she started the car and gunned the engine. Peeling away from the side of the road, she didn't have time to relax. The moment she drove around the bend, she saw the dark pickup truck. And the man striding purposefully toward it.

Her headlights flickered over him, and she caught a better look at his face.

And recognized him. Not by name, but his face. The guy had been at the tavern called Flannery's where she'd met up with Nate to hear the country band. For a split second, their eyes locked before she passed him.

She waited until the man and the truck had disappeared behind her before she pulled out her phone with trembling fingers. Caitlyn quickly dialed 911 but then disconnected before the operator had a chance to answer.

What was her emergency? The woman was dead. The man had killed her. Mesmerized by the man's familiar features, she hadn't even looked at the license plate of the truck.

She inwardly railed at herself for being so stupid. She'd done nothing to help that poor woman, couldn't even find a way to track the man who'd hurt her.

Then again, she hadn't expected the guy to kill the woman. Sure, he'd slapped her, but to kill her? Who did that?

She shivered again despite the heat blowing from the vents. A murder. She'd witnessed a terrible, brutal murder.

The whole thing seemed surreal. Like maybe she'd imagined the entire event. Only she knew she hadn't.

The cat purred again, and she glanced down at the feline's blue eyes. If not for going after this injured kitten, she wouldn't have been there. She struggled to calm her racing heart and thumbed through her directory to find the only cop she knew by name. The man who'd kept her and her sister safe from harm two months ago.

Devon Rainer.

THE RINGING PHONE jarred him from sleep. Twelve forty-five in the morning? Who was calling him at this hour? Grabbing his phone, he blinked the sleep from his eyes to peer at the screen. He'd thought maybe his partner, Bruce Whitmore, was calling, the guy was always arguing with his wife about something, but it was a different name on the screen. He bolted upright in bed. "Hello? Caitlyn? Is something wrong?"

"I-I'm so sorry it's so late, b-but I didn't know who else to call." Her voice was hoarse, as if she'd been crying.

"Are you hurt?" A myriad of possibilities of what may have happened flashed through his mind. "Tell me where you are, I'll come meet you."

"I'm not hurt." She sniffled loudly. "But I saw something terrible. I'm heading toward my apartment, will you please meet me there?"

"Yes, how far away are you?" He pinched the phone between his ear and his shoulder as he pulled on his jeans. Then he reached for his navy blue Sevierville PD sweatshirt. "I can be there in five minutes."

"Thank you. I'll be there about that time too."

He was relieved she wasn't injured, but he was hesitant to disconnect from the call. "Do you want me to stay on the line with you?" Technically, she shouldn't be talking on the phone while driving, but this sounded like an exception to the rule. What terrible thing had she seen?

Meow.

He frowned, still holding on to his sweatshirt. "Is that a cat?"

"Yes, she's wounded. And no, you don't have to stay on the line. I'm only two miles from my apartment building, so could you please hurry?"

"Sure, be there in five." He disconnected from the call, shoved the phone into his pocket, then pulled on his sweatshirt. As Caitlyn was a veterinary technician, he hoped the terrible thing she'd seen wasn't just that someone had hurt the cat.

Like most people, he abhorred animal abuse. There was no reason to hurt a pet. Yet being woken after midnight for such an event seemed a bit extreme. But maybe not to Caitlyn. He knew how much she cared about animals.

Devon pulled on his coat, grabbed his keys, and climbed into his SUV, which was parked in the attached garage. Thanks to the late hour, he made it to Caitlyn's apartment in less than the promised five minutes.

She was waiting for him in her dark gray two-door Honda. When she saw him, she pushed open her door and stood, holding a balled-up red scarf to her chest.

No blood on her face and no evidence of a car crash, so that was good. He crossed over to her. Up close, he could see the small white face of a cat with piercing blue eyes, eerily similar to Caitlyn's, peering out from beneath the red scarf. "What happened? Did someone hurt the cat?"

"Huh? Oh, yes, maybe. I haven't had time to examine her injury." Caitlyn shivered. "Can we go inside to talk? My roommate, Annette, is out of town for two weeks visiting her parents in Florida for the holiday." She glanced around the desolate parking lot. "I'd rather not stay out here."

"Of course." Devon knew Caitlyn well enough to understand she wasn't inviting him in for anything personal. Two months ago, Lincoln Quade had asked him to help protect Caitlyn and her sister, Jayme. At the time, Caitlyn had seemed interested in him. He'd kept his distance, first because he needed to be professional, but more so because despite being drop-dead gorgeous, with her long blond hair and big green eyes, she was too young.

Barely twenty-three to his twenty-eight.

Devon had been involved with Sabrina for three years before she'd left him for another man. One who wasn't a cop because she'd suddenly decided police officers were terrible people riding some big power trip when it came to dealing with the public. *Thanks, media*, he thought sourly.

Since then, he'd kept his relationships light and fun. Easy peasy. No promises of forever.

He'd sensed Caitlyn was a bit naïve when it came to relationships with men. During the short time they'd spent together, he'd learned a little about her past. How she'd spent a couple of years in an abusive foster home before escaping with her older foster sister Jayme thirteen years ago. He'd understood Jayme had protected Caitlyn the best she could from the harsh realities of living on the streets. Admiring what Jayme and Caitlyn had done was easy.

They were both smart and beautiful. But they also were big believers in God, which wasn't really his thing.

"Will you unlock the door for me?" Caitlyn's voice cut into his thoughts.

He took the keys from her shaky hand and did as she'd asked. He held the door for her, then followed her up to her apartment where he unlocked that door too. There were Christmas decorations scattered around the room, including a large fake tree in one corner of the room. It appeared as if Caitlyn was already well into the holiday spirit.

"Thank you." Caitlyn sank down on the sofa, letting out a long sigh. She shifted the scarf-wrapped cat onto the cushion next to her, then ran her finger through her hair. Her face was pale, her gaze cloudy with fear. "Snowball has a laceration that needs attention, but this is more important."

Snowball? He was tempted to smile, but the devastated expression on her face held back the mirth. At least the horrible thing she'd seen didn't involve the cat. He chose to sit on the chair closest to her, reaching out to take her cold hand in his. "What happened, Caitlyn? Why do you look as if you've seen a ghost?"

She stared at their entwined fingers for a moment

before meeting his gaze. "It was worse than that. So much worse."

The tiny hairs on the back of his neck rose in alarm. "Tell me."

She drew in a deep breath. "I—uh, was driving along highway double G, when Snowball streaked across the road in front of me. I caught a glimpse of blood staining her white coat, so I pulled off the road and went looking for her."

He nodded encouragingly. "Apparently, you found her."

"I did. But then I heard arguing between a man and a woman." Her fingers tightened around his. "She was pleading with him, then I heard a slap."

He winced. "Where were they?"

"In the woods." She shook her head. "I know this sounds crazy, but it gets worse."

Worse? In the six years he'd been on the job, he'd seen a lot of bad stuff. People could be so cruel to each other. He forced himself not to overreact. "Go on."

"I—uh, couldn't see them. So I moved farther into the woods. I thought maybe I could interrupt their argument, give the woman time to get away."

Dread coiled in his gut. "Did you find them?"

"Yes." Her voice dropped to a whisper. "But it took me a while to get close enough to see them, and when I looked through the trees, he was—strangling her."

"Strangling her?" He couldn't help but echo what she'd said. "Was she able to get away?"

"No. He must have been choking her for a while because her entire body was limp, but he didn't stop. Not for what seemed like forever. When he finally let her go, she fell to the ground in a heap. Even from a distance, I could see that her eyes were open and staring blankly up at the sky." She paused, gulped, then whispered, "He killed her."

"Did you call 911?"

Caitlyn shook her head. "I was going to once I got back into my car. I started driving. When I came around a curve, I saw the man walking toward his pickup truck. And I recognized him."

"You what?" He jumped to his feet. "Who is he? We need to issue a BOLO for him as soon as possible!"

"No, I don't know his name. I recognized him from Flannery's. He was there tonight, the same way I was." She lifted her tortured gaze to his. "And I think he might have recognized me too."

The chill hardened to ice. "He saw you?"

She gave a jerky nod. "I think so."

He raked his hand through his dark hair and began to pace. "There must be a way to find out who he is. Did you get his license plate number?"

"No." Tears welled in her eyes. "I'm sorry, I know I messed up. But it all happened so fast . . ."

"Shh, it's okay." He reached down to pull her up into his arms. "You didn't mess up. I'm just glad you were able to get away without being hurt." He didn't even want to think about how close Caitlyn had come to being strangled the way the other woman had been.

She buried her face against his chest. After a few minutes, though, she pulled herself together. "I need to look at Snowball's injury and give her food and water."

He glanced down to where the cat was staring up at them. "Okay, but we need to go back to that spot in the woods. Do you think you can find it?"

She stiffened. "Go back? Tonight?"

"Yes." He hated the stark fear in her gaze. "I need to get

the local cops out there too. And a detective. But I think we should find this poor woman first. Keep her safe from predators."

Caitlyn paled but reluctantly nodded. "I just need a few minutes."

He wanted to tell her to leave the cat until they returned, but knowing Caitlyn, she'd refuse. And since he didn't know how long they'd be gone, he let it go.

The dead woman couldn't get any more dead.

True to her word, Caitlyn didn't take long. She carried the cat into the kitchen, talking softly to the animal as she cleaned out her wound. Then she opened a can of tuna and emptied it into a shallow dish. Filling another shallow dish with water, she stood back, watching with satisfaction as the cat began to eat and drink.

"I still need a litter box," she said. After a quick glance around the room, she went over and gathered several potted plants, including a few orchids. She yanked the plants out and tossed them into the garbage. She emptied the containers into a shallow rectangle-shaped pan. She dumped the dirt in first, then layered the bark chips along the top. "It's not kitty litter, but it will have to do."

He lifted a brow. "Won't Annette be upset about the dead plants?"

Caitlyn shrugged. "I'll buy new ones. Besides, if Annette was here, she'd care more about Snowball than a couple of stupid plants."

He suspected she was right. Her roommate was also a veterinary tech at the local veterinary clinic. She was a sweet, attractive kid too. But for some reason, he'd been drawn to Caitlyn.

Too young, he reminded himself firmly. *And far too innocent.*

Caitlyn turned and crossed over to the apartment door. "Let's go."

He followed her out, waiting as she locked the door before they went outside. Cupping her elbow in his hand, he steered her toward his SUV. Glancing at her small Honda, he thought it was a minor miracle that she was able to stay on the twisty mountain highways in that tin can of a car.

"Head toward Knoxville on highway double G," she said once they were settled inside. "This happened about five miles outside of Sevierville."

Five miles might be outside their jurisdiction, but he didn't know that for sure. He hoped the area didn't belong to the park rangers. He cranked the heat and pulled out of the parking lot of her apartment building. A few turns later, they were headed out on highway double G.

He went slow, more so to give Caitlyn the opportunity to recognize the location where this had all taken place. With trees and brush lining both sides of the road, he was concerned that one section of the woods would look just like another.

Would she be able to pinpoint the spot? He hoped so, otherwise he'd be forced to bring half the police department out to search for the poor woman, or what might be left of her, in the morning.

"Slow down," Caitlyn cautioned as she peered past him. He thought they may have to go a few miles out of their way and turn around so that she would be able to see more clearly. "Stop!"

He hit the brakes, harder than he intended, bringing the SUV to a rocking halt. "Where?"

"There, see that small patch of snow in front of that

birch tree?" Caitlyn gestured impatiently. "That's where I went into the woods to find Snowball."

He tried not to let his doubt show on his features. There were many birch trees and several patches of snow. But he had little choice but to give her the benefit of the doubt. "Okay, let's check it out."

She readily jumped out of the car, heading toward the spot she'd indicated. He let her take the lead, hoping they wouldn't get lost.

The path she took was a zigzag pattern. Several times he wanted to ask if she knew where she was going but managed to bite his tongue. She stopped and pointed to a spot near an evergreen tree.

"That's where I found Snowball." She glanced at him. "And where I first heard them arguing."

He swept his gaze over the area. "She's somewhere close by?"

"Not that close. This way." Caitlyn turned and continued walking.

He noticed a few footprints in the snow, indicating she had indeed found the correct location. He wanted to ask how she knew, but she quickened her pace.

"Caitlyn?" He hurried to catch up. She stood in a small clearing, looking frantically around. "Here. She should be right here. Where is she?"

He reached out to grasp her arm. "Calm down, maybe she wasn't dead. Maybe she fell unconscious and managed to get out of the woods on her own."

"No, I saw her eyes. He cut off her air for a long time. I'm telling you, she was dead." Caitlyn waved her arm impatiently. "This is the place it happened, Devon. I know it is."

"I believe you." He blew out a breath. Caitlyn had found this location without any hesitation.

She also claimed she'd witnessed a murder. Yet without a suspect, or a body, there was no proof that a crime had been committed here at all.

Devon scowled. He'd still notify his boss and get a detective assigned to the case, but he had a bad feeling about this.

He was very much afraid this guy might come after Caitlyn next.

Made in the USA
Las Vegas, NV
20 March 2024

87509630R00138